EXPLORATION

AGE OF EXPANSION

EXPLORATION

THE GHOST SQUADRON BOOK 2

SARAH NOFFKE,
MICHAEL ANDERLE

EXPLORATION (this book) is a work of fiction.

All of the characters, organizations, and events portrayed in this novel are either products of the author's imagination or are used fictitiously. Sometimes both.

LMBPN Publishing
PMB 196, 2540 South Maryland Pkwy
Las Vegas, NV 89109

First US edition, December 2017
Version 1.02, February 2018

JIT Beta Readers
From all of us, our deepest gratitude!

Alex Wilson
Belxjander
James Caplan
John Findlay
Kelly O'Donnell
Keith Verret
Kimberly Boyer
Larry Omans
Micky Cocker
Paul Westman
Peter Manis
Sarah Weir
Tim Bischoff

*If we missed anyone, **please** let us know!*

Editor
Jen McDonnell

For Lydia. My greatest treasure in the universe.
-Sarah

To Family, Friends and
Those Who Love
To Read.
May We All Enjoy Grace
To Live the Life We Are
Called.
- Michael

PROLOGUE

General Lance Reynolds' Office, Onyx Station, Paladin System.

"Chief? You there?" asked General Reynolds.

"I'm here. Comms out here aren't secure, but I don't have to tell you that," said Chief Jack Renfro.

"I'll keep it brief," said General Reynolds. He chewed on the end of his stogie, a slight smile on his face. He'd taken to Jack early on. There were very few you could trust when everyone was out to serve themselves or have the Federation serve them. However, Jack Renfro didn't do something to get something. He'd passed up many promotions because they didn't make sense for his real ambition. This was a man who wanted to serve in the right position, not the one that got him a better title and more money. At the core, he had always been a servant to the cause.

"I've got a job for you," said Lance.

"When and where do I need to be?" asked Jack.

"You haven't even heard the details yet." Lance laughed.

"When did that ever matter between the two of us? If you need my help, then I'm there."

"I wouldn't normally ask, but I have a squadron that needs some oversight. I was taking care of it, but I've been pulled away for more...pressing matters. I'm sure you know why and by whom," said Lance.

"I believe I do," responded Jack.

Lance rose and began pacing his office. "Anyway, I wouldn't trust anyone but you to handle this group. They have an incredibly important mission, and I've handpicked them myself. I'm sending over the details of the team right now, along with their previous mission assignments. You'll find that they've been quite busy."

"The report is just coming through. Give me a sec," said Jack, a shuffling sounding over the comms. "Holy shit, General. You can't be serious?"

Lance chuckled. "I'm completely serious. See, I thought you'd have fun with this."

"Those two working together?" he asked. "I'm impressed, boss."

"I'm glad you think so."

"And you've given them the *ArchAngel*?" asked Jack.

"They have an important mission," said Lance.

"Damn, and you even brought back Hatcherick, I see. Damn impressive, sir. Haven't seen a team like this since... well, you know. It's been a *long* time."

"Just wait and see who else I have lined up for this crew," said Lance.

"Don't leave me hanging, boss. Send over the report."

"Does that mean you'll oversee them?" asked Lance.

"I already told you I was committed, and that was before you gave me the details," said Jack.

"I knew I could count on you, Chief," said Lance. "Sending you the rest of the report now. Good luck, Jack."

"Thank you, sir," said Chief Jack Renfro. "It's always an honor to serve."

1

Harbor District. Trinidad City, Axiom 03, Axiom System.

The warehouse was filled with dust and age, the scent of industry still lingering in the air. That was the case with many of the old buildings in this city, ever since the Alegro Corporation packed up its bags and left the system for better financial opportunities. Less money meant less security, which meant more opportunity for criminals.

Captain Edward Teach stood quietly in the middle of the warehouse, waiting for the Trids to unload the merchandise.

"Here you are," said the Trid named Doka. He set a crate down in front of Eddie and stepped back.

Eddie looked to his left at Lars Malseen, a massive Kezzin in full body armor. "Check it."

Lars nodded, bending down to the crate and popping the lock. He opened it, revealing a set of rifles, and took one out to examine it. "Looks good."

"What about the grenades?" asked Eddie, glancing back at Doka.

"All here, all here," Doka assured him. He waved at his associates, who brought three smaller boxes.

Lars checked those, too, and gave Eddie the all-clear.

"Good," said Eddie. "Mind if I ask where you got these?"

"What do you care?" asked the Trid.

"I just like to know where my guns come from."

"From me. That's all you need to know."

"Is it?" asked Eddie. "Because you're the middle man, last I checked."

Doka tapped the small device on his hip, a piece of tech that kept his body hydrated. Trids evolved on an ocean planet and required a very specific chemical to prevent them from drying out. If they went too long without it, they'd die. The device was essential for this reason, as it monitored their vitals and injected the chemical when levels were low. "You insult me," Doka finally said. "That isn't wise."

Eddie chuckled. "Maybe you're right. Sorry, I was just messing around."

"Are you satisfied with these weapons?" asked Doka, who was ready to end this meeting and move on.

"Just about," said Eddie, looking around. "My associate should be here soon to help me square this."

"Your associate?" asked Doka. "You never mentioned—"

"I know, I know. I thought she'd be here by now. I don't know what's taking her so long."

"Maybe she was held up," suggested Lars.

Eddie nodded. "Could be. I guess I could call."

Doka looked at both of them. "What are you talking about? Which one of you has the money?"

Eddie ignored him. "You know, she always does this. I bet she and Hatch are at a bar right now. Probably forgot all about this job."

"I don't think she'd do that," said Lars. "But Hatch might."

"Hey!" barked Doka. "Are you even listening to me?"

Eddie felt his stomach growl. "Speaking of bars, remind me after we're done here to stop and get some grub. I'm fucking starving."

"Me too. I could use a good slab of meat," said Lars, almost drooling at the thought.

Doka snarled, taking a step closer to Eddie. "If you don't tell me right this second what exactly is going on, I'm going to kill both of you and strap your guts to the side of my fucking ship! Are you listening to—"

The door in the back of the warehouse flung open, and an athletic-looking dark haired woman walked in carrying what could only be described as a big fucking gun. She hoisted it up, cocking the rifle, which must have been half her size, with little effort. "Afternoon, boys. What did I miss?"

Doka and his men reached for their weapons. "What's the meaning of this?"

"That's Julianna," explained Eddie. "She can be a little dramatic." He swept beneath his coat and, in a single motion, brought a pistol out and aimed it squarely at Doka's forehead. "She's also my backup."

Doka froze where he stood. "B-Backup?"

"That's right," Julianna said, twisting where she stood

and firing the rifle at the alien to Doka's left. The bullet hit his hand, cutting two of his fingers off and sending the pistol to the floor. The alien screamed in pain.

Lars ran at him, slamming his chest into the alien's, knocking him to the floor.

The thug to Doka's right took this distraction as an opportunity, attempting to shoot Julianna. But Eddie was already prepared. He shot the alien in the leg, downing him, and quickly went for his wrist, grabbing him and twisting, forcing him to let go of the weapon. Eddie pressed his pistol to the thug's forehead. "Easy," he told him. "Don't want to lose your head."

Doka started to back away but froze when he saw Julianna's barrel in his face. She was aiming her massive gun at the arms dealer. "I wouldn't test me, if I were you."

He raised his hands. "O-Okay! I'm sorry!"

Eddie smirked. "Now, that went better than expected." He glanced at the other alien on the floor, who'd just lost two fingers. "Well, maybe not for everyone."

Evidence Locker, QBS *ArchAngel*, Axiom System.

Eddie and Lars were back aboard *the ArchAngel,* stowing the weapons cache they'd collected from the warehouse.

There were at least two hundred small and medium arms, not to mention enough grenades to blow up a small city.

Eddie shoved one of the crates with his foot, pushing it into its designated spot. These still weren't Federation grade weapons. Soon they'd have to steal some advanced guns off of a dumb pirate. It would be a win-win situation.

Shiny new weapons taken from evil aliens. "You think any of these guys got into the whole gun trade thing because they just liked guns?"

"I've never found much success in trying to understand the criminal mind," admitted Lars.

Eddie entered a security code on the crate's lid, locking it down. Then he secured it with a large harness in order to ensure it wouldn't budge later on. "I think most of them are in it for the money, but I bet there's like one or two guys who just enjoy a good gun, you know? Just a couple of halfwits who like to blow shit up."

"You're talking about yourself, aren't you?"

Eddie grinned. "Tell me you don't like it."

"Violence has never been something I take pleasure in," Lars countered. "Though, I will say, there is a certain satisfaction in delivering justice."

"Like today?"

"Especially so," agreed Lars. "We confiscated enough weapons to wage a small war, arrested a dozen criminals, and—"

"And found our target," finished Eddie. He glanced towards the door. "Which, if I'm not mistaken, Julianna is interrogating as we speak."

Interrogation Room, QBS *ArchAngel*, Axiom System.

Julianna slammed Doka against the wall, holding him by his collar. "You'd better tell me what I want to know, bitch-ass, before I get medieval on you!"

"Please don't kill me!" screamed Doka in sheer horror.

Julianna snarled, pressing him further against the wall. "Tell me who your supplier is!"

"I don't know!" insisted Doka. "They have the weapons shipped to us anonymously! We just put the money into an account. I don't know their names!"

She let go, suddenly, and he fell to the floor. "What account?"

He cringed, ducking under his hands. "I-It's a foreign bank. The Trids run it. They have a strict privacy policy, so all the big organizations use them. But I—"

"Give me the account number," ordered Julianna.

He gulped. "I don't know it off the top of my—"

She squatted down and looked him directly in the eyes. "You're going to tell me the number you use," she told him, suddenly calm. "If you don't, I'm going to cut off your leg—" She touched his ankle. "—and I'm going to beat you to death with it."

"Y-You wouldn't really do that…would you?"

"Do you want to find out, Doka?"

He hesitated, then shook his head.

"Good, because I would," she said, matter-of-factly. "And trust me when I tell you, you'd be getting off easy."

"Although I believe you'll keep your word, I can't help you because I don't have the account number memorized."

"Tell me something else then. Tell me where we can find Vas."

Doka blinked up at her, a calm expression on his face. "I can't tell you that either."

Julianna slammed the door to the interrogation room upon exiting. She had to get out of there before she did something she'd regret to the dumb Trid. He wasn't talking, almost like he wanted her to re-arrange his shark face. Ever since seeing those imprisoned by the Brotherhood, she had a new passion to stop them. Julianna had seen it all, but that didn't mean seeing children starved or families separated and imprisoned was something that didn't faze her. She was human after all.

Well, kind of.

Julianna pulled back her fist and launched it at the wall. The force of her punch should have hurt. Would have made a normal person flinch with pain. Julianna only considered doing it again to further relieve the frustration.

"Some things never change," said a voice at her back.

Julianna straightened, tightening her jaw. She turned around, knowing full well who was speaking. "What's that supposed to mean?" asked Julianna, running her eyes over Jack Renfro.

The spymaster for the Federation hadn't changed a bit. Still the same muscular physique and discriminating expression covering his face.

He smirked. "It means, you've still got the same fire I remember."

Julianna allowed herself to grin, her shoulders relaxing. "Some things never die, about like you."

Jack chuckled, a warmth spreading over his features. How long had it been since she'd set eyes on him? A long while, no doubt. "The same could be said about you."

"What brings you aboard the *ArchAngel*?" Julianna asked. One reason she hadn't seen Jack for quite some time was that he had been sent on a series of classified missions. This was a guy who fixed things. Made shit happen. Everyone respected Jack, and those who didn't never stuck around for long.

"I've taken on a new assignment," he responded.

"Oh? General Reynolds hasn't disclosed anything to us," said Julianna, referring to her and Eddie. The *ArchAngel* was under their command and, therefore, anything happening on it should be of knowledge to them.

He nodded. "That's why I'm here. I'm taking over for the general."

2

Bridge, QBS *ArchAngel*, Axiom System.

Eddie was in his quarters when the A.I. pinged to inform him that Julianna had requested his presence. He hoped she'd beaten some useful information out of Doka. So far, they'd had zero leads on where to find Vas since he'd escaped during their battle on the Northern Continent. Usually, a report would have come in through General Reynolds by now, but he'd been unusually quiet since their return.

Strolling through the corridor and onto the bridge, Eddie noticed a stranger beside Julianna. The man stood with his feet shoulder-width apart and hands clasped behind his back, his eyes intently focused on Eddie as he approached.

"Captain Edward Teach, I've heard so much about you," said the stranger, offering his hand to Eddie. "I'm Jack Renfro, and I'll be taking over for General Reynolds as your intelligence liaison."

Eddie eyed the hand for a moment, trying to assimilate this new information. He'd heard of Jack. Hell, most of the Federation had. He just didn't know why the usually private special operations chief would be here. Finally, he shook the man's hand, his chin to the side. "What's happened to the general?"

"He's been pulled away on other business. Lance asked if I would oversee missions for Ghost Squadron in his absence."

Eddie nodded at once, understanding that the most powerful man in the Federation was in high demand. "Pleased to meet you."

Jack seemed to study Eddie for a moment before nodding appreciatively. "I've heard that Ghost Squadron has already had its share of success. It appears you're living up to your reputation, Captain."

"Thank you, sir. I'll do damn near anything to protect our colonies. Scratch that. I'll do *everything*."

"That's why you and Julianna make good partners," said Jack, giving them a slight smile. "Speaking of which, our first order of business is your team. Lance tells me it's severely understaffed."

"Yes, sir," said Eddie. "That's a chief priority of ours. We're currently focusing on hiring pilots, soldiers, and essential personnel."

Jack paused, appearing distracted, his gaze on Julianna. "What is it, Commander Fregin?"

Her eyes dug into the floor as her jaw worked back and forth. "It's that damn Trid we brought in. He knows something and he won't speak up. Vas has him intimidated."

"He might not be of any use to us," said Eddie.

"Or he might know something that gives us an actual lead. What's the point in having a team if we're just going to sit around here and stare at the walls?" fumed Julianna.

Jack took a moment, like he was thinking it over. "You're right," he said after a moment. He sped off in the opposite direction. "I'll be right back."

Eddie watched curiously as Jack left. When he had disappeared, Eddie turned to Julianna. "What do you know about this guy?"

"I know he can be trusted," she answered.

"Anyone who the general put in his place can be trusted," Eddie agreed. "That goes without saying. I was just looking for something a bit more concrete, like who he is and where he came from. You know, details."

"He understands more about what's going on in the Federation than anyone I know, the general being the only exception," she said.

"You're still not telling me anything new," said Eddie.

"If you want to know if he's a Virgo and likes long walks on the beach, then you'll have to ask him yourself." Julianna nodded in Jack's direction as he strode back toward them.

"What's a Virgo?" asked Eddie, genuinely curious.

"Forget it. Doesn't matter right now," she answered.

"Don't pretend like you don't know," muttered Eddie.

Jack cleared his throat when he halted in front of the pair. "I think Doka will be more agreeable to disclosing information to you."

"You spoke with him? Already?" asked Julianna.

"Yes, and I believe you'll have better results this time.

Please, meet me in my office when you're done with the interrogation," he said.

Eddie stifled a laugh. How could he have already gotten that alien to talk? "What did you say to make him open up?" he asked.

"I think you'll find that I have my ways." Jack turned and walked away, leaving the two staring at his backside.

"A man of mystery. I like it," muttered Eddie, elbowing Julianna in the side. "Definitely seems like your kind of guy."

"I don't know what you mean," she answered. "I'm very personable."

Interrogation Room, QBS *ArchAngel*, Axiom System.

A funny expression sat on Doka's face when Julianna and Eddie entered the room. He didn't look in pain but did appear mildly uncomfortable. From what Julianna could tell, there wasn't a mark on the Trid, which meant whatever Jack had done to him didn't involve a physical altercation.

"Okay, we're going to try this again. Do you have an account number to share with us, Doka?" Julianna asked, standing over him.

He shook his large head. "No, I told you I don't remember."

"Why don't you tell me what you *do* remember about Vas before your brains are smashed against the fucking wall?"

Doka gulped. "I don't know where Vas is right now."

Eddie sat down against the table in front of the Trid, his

hands folded casually in his lap. "When you say *right now,* does that mean you know where to find him in the *future?*"

"I, uh, have a meeting with him in two weeks." Doka sounded breathless.

"Where?" asked Julianna, pinning her hands on the table and leaning across it.

"The Harbor District, where I met you but on the south side," said the alien.

"Good, sharky," said Eddie, grinning.

"And what exactly are you giving Vas? What kind of weapons?" asked Julianna.

"I don't have it yet." Doka's eyes twitched. He was shaking.

"*It*? Are you saying that you're delivering a single weapon to Vas?" asked Eddie, his eyebrow arching with curiosity.

Doka nodded furiously. "Right, but I don't have it, and the meeting isn't confirmed until I send word to Vas that it's in my possession."

"What is it that you're supposed to be delivering?" asked Eddie.

Doka's eyes fell to the table, vibrating with fear. "He told me he'd kill me if I leaked any of this information."

A loud sigh tumbled from Julianna's mouth. "Problem is that we'll kill you if you don't tell us. I'm already planning out the most painful death for you as we speak."

Doka shook his head. "You might be tough, but you aren't cruel like Vas."

"Try us." Julianna leaned down low, her knuckles white on the table.

Eddie let out a long and loud yawn. "Look fish-brain,

I'm hungry, wishing I was drunk and, right now, I can't help but think of all that food down in the mess hall. Why don't you tell us what this weapon is you're getting for Vas? We can protect you, put you in witness protection. It doesn't have to be that bad for you."

Doka lifted his chained hands to his gills, which were shivering with…was it fear? Concern? "The truth is, I don't know. I was just told to pick up the weapon and deliver it to Vas."

"Who are you getting this weapon from?" asked Julianna, her tone sharp. "Tell me before you find your head shoved up your ass."

A pained sort of smile formed on the Trid's ugly face. "Ray De'ft. That's the one who—"

"When and where are you meeting?" Julianna's face hovered just in front of the alien's, her eyes burning with intensity.

Doka choked on a breath, his face turning white. He shook his head as he sputtered on a rattled cough.

"Damn it! Tell us what you know about this Ray De'ft. Otherwise, I'm jamming my fist down your throat," threatened Julianna.

"That would be kinder than what'll happen to me if I say any more," answered the Trid.

"Well, torture has a way of making you talk," she said.

"Y-You're correct, which is why I've gone to great lengths to…to avoid that."

Julianna arched her brow at the statement, then shot a glance at Eddie. He shrugged, saying nothing. What could this Trid be talking about? What lengths would he have gone through? He was locked in a cell with only the two of them, so aside from staying quiet, there was nothing he could do.

She moved her foot back, stopping when she felt something on the floor. She glanced down to see an object...one she quickly recognized. It was the device the Trid had been wearing on his hip. The one that ensured he could breathe and didn't dry out in this environment. The device that kept him alive outside of the water. Without this attached to him, he'd be dead in a few minutes.

Julianna lurched for the object, trying to get to it before the worst could happen. As she moved, there came a loud thud. Doka had fallen forward onto the table, his gills no longer fluttering with movement, no longer wet.

The alien was dead and motionless, suffocated from exposure to the air.

3

Jack Renfro's Office, QBS *ArchAngel*, Axiom System

Eddie scratched his chin, his facial hair making it itch. More concerning than his unkempt stubble was the growling in his stomach.

"I don't have any reports on a Ray De'ft," said Jack, scrolling through a pad in his hand.

"Pip also wasn't able to connect this Trid with anyone else," said Julianna.

"Which means we're going to have to do a bit more digging." Jack set the pad on his desk and stared at the two across from him. "This actually leads into one of the first objectives I had for you. I discussed recruitment earlier, you'll recall. What we're going to need now and going forward is someone who can break through different defense networks."

"With all due respect, sir, Pip is equipped to handle such tasks." Julianna was perched on the edge of her seat, her back straight.

He nodded. "He can if he's given the proper proximity to an access point. However, Pip can't do long range infiltrations, and neither can Hatch. What we need is someone proficient at breaking through defense networks. Someone who knows how to hack a conference call or a high-security mainframe. You never know where you'll find the one piece of information you need to connect the other dots. Sometimes, we learn things that are most valuable when taken from the smallest bits of random information."

Eddie leaned forward, his head to the side and a sneaky grin on his face. "Let me guess, you've got someone in mind for that job already."

Jack picked up a folder from the side of his desk and tossed it at the pair. "I do. This civilian has been off the grid for quite some time and wasn't even an option until recently. However, I think we now have the right resources to locate and bring him in."

"What resources would that be?" asked Julianna, eyeing Eddie as he flipped open the folder.

"Doctor A'Din Hatcherik," said Jack. "The squid you both have come to know so well."

"Why is he the key? How can he help us?" asked Julianna.

"He has a history with hacking under his alias, Brody Chambers. That name has garnered some respect among hackers on the Dark Web. Before recently, Hatch wasn't with the Federation and, therefore, not in the position to assist us with identifying our target and locating him. However, now that he has joined your squad, he should be more than willing to help you."

"Chester Wilkerson," Eddie read from the file. "Independent contractor responsible for hacking into several terrorist defense networks. He definitely sounds like our kind of guy. Why can't you get ahold of him?"

"His work with the Federation led to problems, both directly and indirectly. According to the report, he was compromised when his work led to threats against his life from a certain terrorist organization. He's now living on Kemp in the Behemoth system, avoiding detection as best he can. He trusts no one, not even the Federation."

"Ugh, that's way the fuck out there, the same place where we picked up Hatch. What's up with these guys relocating out to these shitty planets?" asked Eddie.

"If you don't want to be found, go to a place where no one wants to visit," said Julianna, tugging the folder out of Eddie's hands.

"The report doesn't tell us what city he's in, or even what continent." Eddie threw a thumb in the direction of the folder. "All it says is he's suspected to be on that planet."

"That's because we don't know. Honestly, we're guessing on Kemp. What little information we have was grabbed from brief online interactions. What we need is someone to get in contact with Chester and trace his location remotely."

Eddie smiled. "That's why you need Hatch."

"Exactly right."

"But why can't Hatch just do the hacking for us?" asked Eddie.

Jack shook his head. "Hatch is impressive, but we need someone with specialized knowledge of the Trid network. I believe Hatch has the skills to pull this guy out of hiding, but he can't do what he does."

Julianna slapped the file on the desk, her face serious. "Let's suppose that Hatch *can* locate Chester in a chat group and trace his location. How do you know if we go after him that he'll agree to work for us? He's in hiding for a reason."

Jack tapped his fingers rhythmically on the desk while he thought. "That's a good question. Chester used to be an independent contractor, working for the Federation out of his apartment. One day, a group of terrorists got wind of his location and stormed in after him. He got away, but only barely, as I understand it. He's probably been running ever since. I'm guessing he's going to prefer a job where he's actually protected on the *ArchAngel* rather than whatever one has him skipping locations on rundown planets. Give him that offer, and maybe he'll take it. Hell, maybe you can offer to help him clean up this mess he's gotten himself into."

"However..." Eddie said, sensing the word about to come.

Jack nodded, his expression apprehensive. "However, getting to Chester is going to be the challenge. We tried to bring him in at first, but he was so fearful of terrorists he started running until he was off the radar. He's paranoid, and with good reason. There are those out there who still want to punish him for leaking their data. Furthermore, there's others who would love to get their hands on a hacker like Chester just to use him. This isn't just a damn good hacker, but one of the very best in the entire Federation. Whoever has him on their side is in a prime position to win over their enemy. Information is power, and Chester knows how to siphon that from just about any organization."

"Sounds like we need this guy on our team. Let's get Hatch to work on it immediately," said Eddie, getting to his feet. "Time to put this plan of yours into motion.

Dining Hall 03, QBS *ArchAngel*, Axiom System

Eddie took three bites of his salami sandwich before chewing. His cheeks were full, the food nearly spilling out of his mouth. He washed it down with a few sips of beer, wiping his chin with his sleeve.

"Only for the Federation would I willfully starve myself," said Eddie, looking across the table at Lars.

The alien eyed the sandwich in Eddie's hands like it was disgusting garbage. "I didn't know you were ordered to starve yourself, sir."

Eddie laughed, taking another sip of beer. "I wasn't. Just been too damn busy to eat sorting through files of potential recruits. How's flight training going?"

"It's good. I'm enjoying it. Flying feels much more natural than I thought it would."

Eddie smiled, remembering when he first started flying. Before that, his life was dull and meaningless. Then, like a breath of fresh air, he had found purpose, fulfillment. He'd found himself, there in the depths of space, flying among the stars. He would never forget that feeling.

The feeling of being truly free.

It was hard to believe that before Julianna and Lance had recruited him that he had settled for a life without his wings. "The thrills you get while flying…they can't be matched by anything," Eddie finally said. "Well, almost, if you know what I mean."

He grinned.

"Hatch says he's working on building a new Q-Ship, since the other one was destroyed," Lars said, apparently not getting Eddie's joke.

"Yeah, the poor guy isn't dealing well with the loss of his ship." A burp ripped out of Eddie's lips before he took another bite of the sandwich.

Lars eyed the food, then shook his head. "That stuff covering the meat, what is it?"

"Bread," supplied Eddie. "It's the delivery device for the goodness inside the sandwich."

"Why don't you just eat the meat? That…bread…doesn't look very tasty."

"Says someone who can't process anything but meat." Eddie shook his head, showing Lars his sandwich. "My friend, everything tastes better on bread. Sandwiches have to be the best invention ever. If humanity were better, we would build statues to the person responsible for its deliciousness."

"If you say so." Lars stared down at the untouched roasted chicken on his plate.

"Hey, what's up? Is it flight training? You nervous about it?" Eddie wasn't necessarily a sensitive person, but he was observant enough to tell when his teammate was uneasy.

"No, flight training is fine. It's a distraction. It's exactly what I need."

"Is it…your family?" guessed Eddie.

"I do think of them often. I worry for them, but that hasn't really changed since the Brotherhood took me.

Those living on Kezza have been in danger for a long time."

"I told you I'd help you get back there. I wasn't blowing smoke. If you want to leave then—"

"I don't want to leave. If I return to Kezza, then I won't be in a better position to help my family. The place for me to do that is here, working for you. That's the decision I've made."

Eddie nodded, polishing off the last of his sandwich. "We're going to get you home one of these days, when it makes sense."

"I know you will. I've never doubted that. I thought about returning. Really thought about it. I was ready to do it. Then we learned more about the Brotherhood, and I couldn't just run back home."

"Yeah, I was surprised the Brotherhood abandoned all their old locations after Commander Orsa's capture. Just means they're scared," said Eddie, furrowing his brow. "Damn straight, too. They should be."

"Do we know anything about whoever they got to replace him?" Lars asked. His tone was insistent, like he needed to know.

"Not yet, but we will." Eddie pointed at the chicken in front of Lars. "Starving yourself isn't the way. Eat up, big guy. I need you to be ready."

Hatch waddled over to one of his many workstations. This one wasn't cluttered with parts and materials for the Q-Ship he was working on. A keyboard and six screens sat on the desk. Hatch slid onto the chair, his tentacle gliding over the keys, typing in his password.

"How do you plan to draw the hacker out?" asked Pip, his voice sounding from overhead.

"Oh, what's with the questions? Wouldn't you rather be surprised?" asked Hatch.

"Surprised? I'm not sure that's possible," said Pip.

"There's all sorts of possibilities now that you've been upgraded." Hatch typed on the keyboard, opening a few different screens.

"I do notice differences since the upgrade, but surprise hasn't been one of them."

"Be sure to catalogue all changes. I want to review them at some point. Maybe make adjustments," said Hatch.

"So that I can better help the team?" asked Pip.

"Yes, there is that," agreed Hatch.

"I sense that there is something you're not saying."

"There are many things I'm not saying, mostly because I'm trying to concentrate." Hatch typed rapidly, entering numerous backdoors inside a secret network. The Oddframe was a forum where many hackers were known to convene. The right person could access illegal torrents, find untraditional programming solutions, or buy prohibited software. Hatch entered a hidden chat group, one that he'd been searching for on-and-off throughout the day.

He waited until his cursor popped up beside his username.

BRODY CHAMBERS: Infected with a heisenbug by a damn blackhat. Looking for a solution.

Three other usernames popped up with comments.

"I'm running a search on these hacker terms. Blackhat refers to a malicious hacker, correct?" asked Pip.

"Correct," chirped Hatch. "And heisenbug is a particularly nasty virus that usually goes undetected when debugged programs are run. They are incredibly tough to get rid of because they have time to hose the mainframe before detection."

Hatch scanned the responses, hoping one would stand out as belonging to Chester Wilkerson. He'd chatted with the famous hacker once or twice, he believed, but only deduced that based on his incredible knowledge.

FROGS MCGRILLS: Brods! where you been?

ZOOM LOCKES: blackhats need to die!!!

MONTE NILES: when/where did you get the virus?

"This looks promising." Hatch shut down a few of the other windows where he'd been asking the same question. He recognized Monte.

BRODY CHAMBERS: @Monte idk. You have a fix for the newest strand?

A few more users chimed in, most of them welcoming Brody back. He'd been gone for a long time.

MONTE NILES: I might. Depends…

Hatch opened a new window and sent a direct message to Monte Niles.

"You believe that Monte is Chester, correct?" asked Pip.

"Yes, I've chatted with him before. His knowledge is unmatched. I've searched eighty-five chat rooms and he's finally popped up."

BRODY CHAMBERS: Hey @Monte. Been thru every link farm and can't find fix. Got one?

MONTE NILES: I was under the impression that you could fix most heisenbugs. Things change?

"He's doubting you, is that right?" asked Pip.

"Yeah, damn my brilliance. I've always been the one to offer solutions. He's finding it hard to believe that I can't solve the current version of a heisenbug."

"You can fix a heisenbug?" asked Pip.

"With all my tentacles tied behind my back and blindfolded," said Hatch.

"How do you plan to fool this Monte Niles?"

"Chester, you mean," corrected Hatch. "But I don't need to fool him. All I have to do is keep him in this private chat a little longer. The tracker is already searching for his current location, but it will only work for as long as he has this private message window opened."

"Wouldn't Chester have systems to detect trackers?" asked Pip.

"He absolutely will have, and furthermore, he's able to hide the amount of power he's using, which would be a bull's eye on planet Kemp. However, I've got a tiny window to find a huge source of power, and that should lead us straight to Mr. Hacker."

Two of Hatch's tentacles typed on the keyboard, cycling through the different images on the screens as the tracker processed.

BRODY CHAMBERS: Might be screwage rather than bug. Any clues?

A long moment passed where Hatch simply stared at the screen, waiting, hoping for a reply. He tapped one tentacle on the workstation impatiently.

"Fifty seconds until trace is complete," informed Pip.

"We'll get him. Just have to ensure he doesn't drop off."

MONTE NILES: Sending over file. Should work

A file followed Monte's message. One that no doubt would fix the bug if Hatch actually had one.

BRODY CHAMBERS: Thanks. You're a lifesaver.

MONTE NILES: Didn't realize it was that serious

BRODY CHAMBERS: You know how it goes

MONTE NILES: Hope it works. I'm off

"Oh no! He can't be off," said Hatch.

"The trace hasn't completed," said Pip.

BRODY CHAMBERS: Wait. Another question...

"You're stalling," observed Pip.

"I'm trying," Hatch snapped.

MONTE NILES: What?

BRODY CHAMBERS: I actually didn't need a fix to for a heisenbug

MONTE NILES: No kidding...

"You're confessing. I don't understand," said Pip.

"I'm stalling, but more importantly, I'm using some honesty to get what I need."

"He could run, though," said Pip.

"He could, but not if I'm fast." Now three of Hatch's tentacles typed away at the keyboard.

BRODY CHAMBERS: I need a custom hack

MONTE NILES: Why?

BRODY CHAMBERS: Because you're the best

MONTE NILES: You lured me into chat for this?

BRODY CHAMBERS: Willing to pay. My bitcoin account is full

A long, excruciating few seconds passed where Monte, AKA Chester, didn't respond.

"The trace hit a snag. We need him connected for twenty more seconds," said Pip.

"I don't know," muttered Hatch. "This guy may not want money. He might just prefer to stay alive."

"Life has not always appeared more important than money, my records show," said Pip.

"It should. Can't buy a damn thing if we're dead." Hatch drummed two tentacles on the desk impatiently. "Come on, Chester. You have to eat. Bite, would you?"

MONTE NILES: What are you looking for?

Hatch puffed out his cheeks, both relieved and excited. "Yeah, he's hungry. I knew he had to be."

"Trace complete. We have a location," said Pip.

BRODY CHAMBERS: Oh, I just found it. Never mind. Thanks.

MONTE NILES: Okay. Maybe next time.

Hatch closed the browser window, letting out a long breath.

4

Loading Dock 04, QBS *ArchAngel*, Axiom System.

Eddie picked a blue marble off the table where Hatch was working under a frame of a new ship. He tossed the marble high in the air, catching it softly with the palm of his hand. Julianna joined him on one side, a curious look on her face as she eyed him tossing the marble.

"Do you think that's wise?" she asked.

Eddie raised the marble to his eye. "Yeah, I think I can handle this little ball of glass, but thanks for the concern, doll-face."

"It appears that someone wants to lose their left testicle," she remarked, raising her brow.

Eddie laughed. "That's specific. Why are you going after the left one? Why not both? Or the right?"

"I was under the impression you didn't have both to spare," she said.

Both Eddie's eyebrows raised with alarm. "Damn, Federation reports are fucking specific."

"Yes, we have ways of knowing things."

Hatch rolled out from under the frame of the new Q-Ship, standing upright and blossoming out to his usual size. "Oh, good, you're here. I have some technology for you that will prove useful for your mission to bring in Chester Wilkerson."

"Not sure why a skinny hacker requires special weapons, but I'll never turn down a bigger gun." Eddie strolled after Hatch who waddled in the opposite direction.

"You've obviously never been to the planet Kemp," said Julianna.

"That, I haven't."

"And don't underestimate a hacker, especially one like Chester. Bringing him in will warrant new weapons, ones that guns won't work for."

Hatch picked up a black piece of clothing from the work table and held it in the air. The material was reflective but appeared light as it dangled down. "Kemp is known for its random air raid attacks as well as mines and bombings. Pip should be able to locate some of the bombs on the ground but, unfortunately, the threat is too high. This is going to be your insurance."

"A cool new shirt. Why thank you, buddy, but I think I'll stick with my armor," said Eddie.

"You can stay with your heavy armor that weighs you down and only covers your torso or you can graduate to this." Hatch used another of his tentacles to stretch out the material to reveal a long-sleeved shirt.

"Did you go into fashion design or have you something else up your sleeve?" Eddie asked, jokingly.

Hatch and Julianna didn't laugh.

"This is a new armor I've invented. It's as light as cotton, covers more area, breathes easily, and can stop ten times the impact of the shit you've been using," said Hatch.

"That's brilliant, Hatch," said Julianna.

Hatch beamed, his face seeming to puff a bit.

"You're telling me that this piece of cloth is actually armor?" asked Eddie, reaching out and taking it from Hatch and examining it.

"Indeed. Just imagine when I figure out how to equip the Q-Ship with something just like it, only it'll be capable of stopping a torpedo instead of just a bullet." Hatch's cheeks puffed again. "Oh, I can't wait for that."

"We'll be light as hell. No one will catch us," said Eddie enthusiastically.

"This is great news, Hatch. New armor for us and one day for the new Q-Ships," said Julianna.

"I don't know when the new ship will be ready. There's a few obstacles I'm dealing with, but that's not your concern right now. What you need is weaponry for Kemp." Hatch shuffled over to a different table, his eyes distant.

Eddie scratched his cheek. "What do you know about Kemp, besides the whole bombing problem?"

Hatch shrugged. "It's right beside Ronin, so I know more than I like. This isn't a place anyone goes to vacation. Rundown isn't the right word for it. That's what they'd say about Ronin. Kemp is more a wasteland. It's overrun with different outlaw gangs. If you can't make it as a pirate, you end up on that planet."

"Didn't think pirates had such high standards," remarked Eddie.

"You'd be surprised how much goes into successfully

pillaging an area," replied Hatch. He picked up a bag made from the same black material as the armor. "Now, let's discuss weapons. You're heading over in the transport ship, which means you can't bring the artillery arsenal on the Q-Ship."

"Jack said you needed us to keep the Q-Ship here so you could copy its system," said Julianna.

"Not really copy as much as reference. That one is a copy itself, and I'm trying to replicate the original, which was superior to the only existing Q-Ship," explained Hatch

"I like the idea of small weapons we can carry on transport ships." Eddie tossed the marble he'd been carrying underhanded into the air and caught it.

"Then might I suggest you put that grenade down before you knock yourself out," spat Hatch.

Eddie froze, opened his hand, and stared down at the blue marble sitting innocently in the palm of his hand. "This…this is a grenade?"

"Yes, it is. More specifically, *that* one is a concussion grenade." Hatch's tentacle stretched forward until its end wrapped around the marble in Eddie's hand, snatching it away.

Eddie's eyes widened. "You've got my attention. Breathable shirts that act as armor and marbles that blow shit up. You're one crafty octopus."

Julianna cast an annoyed look at him before shaking her head and returning her attention to Hatch. "That bag, is it full of these grenades?"

"It is, but the bag is made from the same material as the armor, so no worries about an accidental detonation." Hatch's tentacle slithered into the opening of the bag and retrieved a blue marble. "The marbles are divided in half by a single line." He held the orb out for Julianna to examine.

She took it and spied the fine line around its center.

"When you want to detonate the grenade, simply twist the separate halves in opposite directions. Then, you toss." Hatch reached into the bag and pulled out another orb. Red, this time. "Captain, since you're an idiot who can't keep things straight, I've color-coded the grenades. You can thank me at your leisure."

"Why, thank you!" Eddie grinned, rocking forward on his toes and back down to his heels.

"The blue ones are concussion grenades, perfect for smaller areas." Hatch held the red marble up in one tentacle. "The red ones are explosive grenades, capable of destroying anything in a three to four foot radius. Not deadly, but a good distraction if necessary."

"Not bad at all for a tiny bag we can carry on our hip," said Eddie.

"Thanks, Hatch. These are great and will definitely help us on Kemp." Jules reached out and took the small bag from the alien. He smiled appreciatively, turning pink around the cheeks.

Main Cabin, Transport Ship, Axiom System.

"Isn't it funny that we find ourselves back on this transport ship headed back to Behemoth system?" asked Eddie.

"Your sense of humor is lacking." Julianna stretched into one of the reclining chairs in the main cabin. Again, they had it to themselves, another perk of working for the Federation.

"Hey, Lars, guess what?" Eddie called to the alien who was just entering the cabin, staring around, taking in the shiny recliners and polished surfaces.

"What am I guessing?" asked Lars.

Eddie laughed. "I don't really have something for you to guess. I just wanted to get your attention."

Lars took the seat next to the captain. "Okay, you have it."

"Everything on the transport ship is comped. How cool is that?"

Julianna rolled her eyes, lifting a pad in front of her face and reading the screen.

Lars blinked dully at the captain. "I'm not sure if I fully understand. I've been fortunate enough to have the Federation pay for all of my supplies, as well as my boarding. Why should I be more grateful in this situation?"

Eddie threw his head back, momentarily frustrated by his traveling companion. "My poor sweet Lars, you innocent bastard. You've been fortunate enough to have your needs met, this is true, but now we're talking *luxury*, brother." He waved down the flight attendant, requesting her pad, which she gave freely to him. Eddie pointed to the screen, tapping it several times, and then handed it to Lars. "I'll be having *that*. Now, you order." He lifted his chin in Julianna's direction. "Don't worry, I ordered your usual. You're welcome."

She lowered the pad so only her eyes were visible. "Remember what happened last time?"

Eddie grinned. "I do. We had a fantastic time. Eh, but don't worry, I'm not planning on repeating that. I only ordered half the drinks for me. You'll get your full bottle of whiskey, though."

Lars dropped the pad, looking stunned. "Commander Fregin drank an entire bottle of whiskey?"

"A bit more, if we're getting specific," said Eddie. "But who's counting?" He waved his hand through the air dismissively.

"This isn't like last time where we were retrieving a cooperative Londil," reminded Julianna.

"Which is why I've scaled back my drink order. You've got to live a little. Remember how much fun you had? Drinks, steak, chocolate cake," said Eddie.

Julianna's eyes sparkled for a moment with the memory. "The cake was something else. Yes, I'll take a piece of that," she said to the flight attendant.

"Of course, ma'am," confirmed the woman.

"Cake?" asked Lars, still browsing through the menu.

"Unfortunately, you wouldn't like cake. It would probably kill you." Eddie turned to the flight attendant. "We'll take two steaks and whatever drinks my friend likes."

"Just bring me whatever he's having." Lars pointed to Eddie.

Julianna slipped low in her own seat, getting comfortable. "That might not have been a good idea unless you want to sleep the rest of the journey. Eddie's a lush."

"A lush?" asked Lars.

"Don't listen to her, Lars," said Eddie. "She's just upset that it takes a bottle of whiskey for her to get buzzed. All those genetic enhancements, ya know."

"Ah," said Lars, glancing at Julianna. "A blessing and a curse."

Eddie frowned, then shook his head. "Such a shame."

"That's impossible. You really don't age?" Lars asked, his eyes drooping slightly from the Blue Ale.

Julianna threw back another shot of whiskey. "I do, but not as fast. Nano technology made it so that my human body was enhanced. I'm the optimal height, build, and weight. I can be injured, but my body repairs itself incredibly fast."

"And she can't get drunk as easily. Talk about sad," said Eddie, holding his glass in his hand and pointing in Julianna's direction with his pinky finger.

"I had no idea any of this was possible," said Lars, his eyes large with amazement.

"The Federation makes all sorts of things possible." Eddie cut into his steak, his mouth salivating from the ease of which his knife sunk into the flesh.

Lars did the same, and they both looked at each other as they lifted the meat to their mouths. Both let out sounds of pleasure.

"I've rarely tasted anything so good," said Lars.

"I told you, man," replied Eddie.

"And here I thought you were incapable of enjoying a good meal, you ugly human." Lars laughed, his lizard face pink from the alcohol.

"I can enjoy all sorts of meals. It just so happens I prefer a potato with my steak."

Lars eyed the vegetable sitting alongside Eddie's steak.

"I don't get that part, but I'm glad we both can enjoy the meat together."

"Cheers to that." Eddie lifted his glass and held it out to Lars. They clinked their glasses, and Julianna held hers in their direction, nodding appreciatively just as the transport ship shifted into landing mode.

Mabank City, Kemp. Behemoth System.

"Looky there. I had an all access pass to food and drink and I didn't get wasted. You should be proud of me." Eddie threw a glance backwards at Julianna.

"I hope you're not looking for a medal because you're not getting one."

"That's where you're wrong," remarked Eddie. "I'll get one still. Just you wait."

Lars paused outside the transport ship and stared around. "Are we in the right place?"

"I'm afraid so," Julianna said from over his shoulder. Mabank was mostly an assortment of murky grays, its buildings wrought by years of warfare and poverty. The economy had tanked many decades ago, and now the city was host to disease and low life scum who couldn't make it anywhere else. A low-flying aircraft, which looked like it might fall out of the sky at any moment, roared overhead.

Lars covered his ears. "Where are we headed?"

"To the middle of BFE," said Julianna.

"What's BFE?" asked Lars.

"Bum Fucking Egypt. It's an old human expression that means the middle of nowhere," she explained.

Lars tilted his head. "I thought we already were in BFE."

He glanced around at the tiny airport, most of which was filled with crop duster planes.

"You'd be surprised how much worse it's going to get," said Julianna.

Eddie flagged down another Kezzin, who was standing off to the side by himself. A moment later, Eddie pressed his thumb to a pad and handed it back to the alien, then received a set of keys.

When he returned, he was smiling. "I called ahead and reserved us a vehicle," said Eddie.

Julianna nodded, then loaded into the front of the vehicle. "You have your moments, but don't break your arm patting yourself on your back." She took out her pad, pulling up the directions. "We're headed north. Let's get going."

"So damn bossy," said Eddie, chuckling. He turned the key and started the engine. "Alright, folks. Let's go explore us a city!"

"Nothing like driving a rundown piece of shit to make you appreciate your Q-Ship," said Eddie as they cruised down a dirt road.

"Yes, my appreciation is high right now." Lars covered his head, which kept careening into the overhead in the back every time they hit a large bump.

Overgrown fields of corn ran the length of the road and stretched out in all directions. Those plants were Mabank's currency. A fucking vegetable. It could be used for everything from fuel to food, but the planet had failed the export negotiations, losing many of the larger contracts. Now, the city of Mabank and its surrounding areas had corn coming out of their asses and no one to sell it to. That's why the town had been overrun by pirates and gangs and was often victim to attacks.

"Hold on to your butts. Got another pothole coming up," boomed Eddie, trying to swerve the car. The vehicle reacted a bit slowly.

"That was more of a crater, I'd say." Julianna bounced, keeping her eyes fixed on the farm houses sprinkling the distant fields.

"What's the plan?" Lars asked from the back.

"Chester, according to Hatch's tracking, lives in an apartment building in town, a mile up ahead. With any luck, he won't be expecting us. Lars, you take the rear in case he tries to flee. Jules and I will take the main entrance."

"Hard to believe there's a town in all of this corn," said Julianna, staring out at the field.

"I hear if you blink, you'll miss it." Eddie laughed, slowing the jeep after having caught up with a slow-moving tractor that was hogging the road. It was probably made using plans from Earth, since it looked to have a similar design. "Fuck, come on with this shit."

"How do you like that?" asked Julianna. "Travel halfway across a galaxy, only to get held up by a damn tractor."

The old farmer slowed more, pulling the tractor over into the ditch to allow the car to pass. Eddie waved at the man, who looked all too displeased to see them kicking up dust on the old road.

Ahead, the road evened out and led into a small town, where squatty buildings lined the main street. Dirty men sat on the curb, staring blankly at their feet or lying on broken benches.

Julianna pointed to a parking space. "The apartment building is a road over from here. I say we park on this street and walk through the alley so we don't draw attention to ourselves pulling up."

"Right, let's not draw attention to ourselves..." Eddie motioned to their shiny black uniform and holstered weapons. "We wouldn't want to do *that*."

The three slid through a narrow alleyway that smelled of ash and smoke. Their boots trampled over broken glass and other debris. At the exit to the alley, Eddie motioned to Lars to go around the back of the building. It was five stories tall and made of brown brick. There, on a stoop, a man sat by himself, whittling a stick.

"Oh, looks like old Chester will be moving again," the man said when he looked up at Eddie and Julianna. "That's oh-so sad."

"You know Chester? We're not here to hurt him. Quite the opposite," said Eddie, looking down at the old man who had one blind eye.

"No one knows Chester," he said, his one good eye watching his stick.

"He's on the third floor," muttered Julianna to Eddie, striding forward into the apartment building. The sounds of babies crying, husbands yelling, and feet stomping echoed from inside the cavernous apartment building. They charged up the stairs, stopping once they reached the third floor. The first two doors in the hallway were ajar, by the look of them, but the third and final door was shut.

"I pick door number three." Eddie strode forward, his shoulders held back.

"Wait," whispered Julianna. She pulled the flashlight from her belt and switched the setting on it down two clicks. When she turned it on, the black light revealed a set of laser beams that stretched across the hallway, making an obstacle course of sorts.

"What's all this?" asked Eddie.

"Looks like a security system," she answered.

"Why would he have a security system in the middle of a hallway? Wouldn't the other people living here trigger it?" he asked.

Julianna paused, growing very still. "There's no one else here," she muttered, staring with distant eyes. "Most of the floor is empty."

"How can you tell?" asked Eddie.

She relaxed, like she'd come out of a trance. "I have good ears."

Eddie cocked his head. "Was that one of your abilities?"

She nodded. "Something like that."

"I never knew you had fancy hearing like that," he said.

"I have to concentrate to use it, and it doesn't work if there's gunfire or a ton of noise," she explained.

"Nice, but it doesn't solve this problem," said Eddie. "What should we do? Fuck if our hacker hasn't thought of everything."

"Actually, I'm sure he has more in store for us if we trigger one of those lasers," remarked Julianna.

"Like an anvil to the head." Eddie pointed up to the ceiling where something was suspended overhead, too hard to make out in the darkened space.

"This isn't a cartoon," said Julianna. "Most likely, it'll be a bomb beneath one of the floorboards."

Eddie gulped. "Yikes."

Julianna nodded. "You hold the light for me. I think I have the best chances of making it through this maze of lights." She got down low, pressing her chest to the dusty floor and scooting forward until she'd cleared the first laser. The next bit required her to high step, weave her body through the obstacle course, and finally lean down low as she side-stepped between two tight lasers.

Eddie watched from afar as the genetically modified supersoldier made it look easy.

"Awesome," whispered Eddie, still holding the flash light.

"Actually, I'm surprised it wasn't more difficult," said Julianna. "Which is what bothers me."

"Try not to be so cynical," said Eddie. "You did great!"

Julianna dismissed him with a shake of her head, quietly pointing to a camera in the corner.

"Maybe you can try talking to him through that," said Eddie.

Julianna turned and faced the camera. "Chester Wilkerson, I'm Commander—"

An ear-splitting beep rang out from a speaker under the camera. It made Julianna and Eddie double over at once, clapping their hands to their ears. The sounds jolted Eddie straight in the teeth, vibrating his skull. It wasn't even a loud sound, just an ungodly one. He managed to reach for the pistol in his belt and hold it up, aiming it at the speaker, although his hand was shaking from the excruciating sound. He fired and the sound dissipated, breaking at last.

"Fuck! That made my jaw come unhinged." Eddie grabbed his chin and toggled it back and forth, trying to release the strange pressure in his head.

"Yeah, you're telling me. So much for trying the welcoming approach." Julianna knocked at the door in front of her and suddenly convulsed, electronic shocks started at her fist and wrapped around her arm. She yanked herself backward, eyeing the door with great offense. "Damn it! This guy is fucking insane. He better be worth all this."

"If he isn't, then you can use him as a sparring dummy."

Julianna agreed with a nod, pulling her own pistol from her harness, and firing it at the locks on the door. It creaked open an inch, the locks having been broken. She picked up her foot and knocked the rubber bottom into the door, sending it back all the way. With her gun at the ready, Eddie watched her enter the apartment, his eyes intently on her. He felt trapped on the far side of the hallway, but those lasers triggered something, or a whole host of somethings, and he wasn't going to chance that until he had to.

"We have a runner!" yelled Julianna, sprinting back out into the hallway. "He's taking the fire escape down!" She ran across the hallway, triggering multiple traps, ignoring the lasers. Heavy objects rained down from the ceiling and catapulted from the open doors of the other apartments.

She slipped by each of them, making it back to the far end of the hallway where Eddie had been standing. "Holy shit!" he barked.

"I know!" she answered.

"He really did put stuff in the ceiling!" he exclaimed.

"Who even does that?"

"Hurry! He's getting away!" said Julianna.

Eddie bolted, leaping down the stairs, taking them five at a time until both he and Julianna were out into the open air in front of the apartment building.

Lars stood with his back against the metal walls of a warehouse, his eyes scanning the back of the apartment. He spotted a young human pop his head out of the third story window, just before he heard Julianna yell from inside the building. Lars' sprinted forward, about to leap onto the fire escape. This was his chance to help the team bring in Chester. The guy he was supposing was the hacker in question had something in his hands, a metal object of some sorts.

Lars was up the first floor of the fire escape when he looked up. This was too easy. He'd meet Chester on the way down and subdue him until Eddie and Julianna arrived. Then they could be out of there and off Kemp, which smelled like a pile of burning garbage.

He glanced up when he'd nearly cleared the second floor. Chester had positioned the metal object onto a wire that was bolted into the side of the building. He held on to either side of the wire, then kicked off. Easily, he glided across the alleyway, down and to the warehouse on the other side. He dropped, sliding to the ground when he was close enough to land.

"Damn it!" sputtered Lars. He threw himself over the railing and landed, rolling out of the jump to lessen the impact of the fall. Lars sprang forward and sprinted after Chester, who had entered the warehouse from a small side door. He caught up quickly, reaching the warehouse in record time.

Inside, it was dark and smelled of moldy dust. Lars slowed to a walk as he became more mindful of potential ambushes, staring up at the tall shelves, each filled with dozens of crates. Chester could be anywhere, for all he knew, or he could have run through the place entirely and be on the other side by now.

Lars stepped carefully, his senses working overtime to try and find any clue that told him where the hacker was hiding.

"We're not here to hurt you. Just come out and we can talk," said Lars, staring up at the shelves that reached the ceiling.

In front of Lars came a shuffling noise. He spun around. A dragging sound. He squinted in the darkened warehouse, up at the shelf where the noise was emanating.

A large crate fell forward, toppling overhead to the floor where Lars stood. He dived just in time to avoid being crushed by the crate, which busted upon impact, its bits of wood spraying in all directions. Lars' covered his head, continuing to run forward.

Another crate fell from even closer, that one nearly landing on Lars' as well. He picked up the pace and sprinted down the length of the row until he was on the far end. Three more crates had fallen. Chester must be on the third shelf, pushing the crates out.

Lars dove to the left, looking up at the third shelf. He could barely make out the figure running in the opposite direction, along the length of the shelf. Dashing forward, Lars ran down the side of the warehouse, hoping to cut Chester off.

Eddie had spied Lars entering the warehouse just as he'd come around the building. Julianna took the side entrance, and he sped past her, taking the main one on the other side.

He was just about to jerk the door back when he heard footsteps slapping against the concrete. Pulling his gun from his holster, he took a steady breath. No, he didn't want to point a weapon at a potential teammate. However, Chester was scared and didn't know who they were. That was a deadly combination, and Eddie couldn't take a chance on him just yet.

He yanked the warehouse door open and slid into the open space, gun at the ready. A guy came running forward, his head turned to look over his shoulder as he cleared the space. He spun his head forward and halted at the sight of Eddie standing squarely in the doorframe, gun pointed at him.

Chester spun to face the side entrance just as Julianna stepped out from a row, her gun pointed at him. The guy turned, putting his back to Eddie. To his relief, Lars approached from the back, his own weapon held up, pointed at Chester. The hacker spun around until he was facing Eddie once again.

"I'm Captain Edward Teach, and I'm here to offer you a job," said Eddie, lowering his weapon.

5

Storage Warehouse, Mabank City, Kemp. Behemoth System.

Chester Wilkerson held up his hands, his brown eyes flicked between Eddie and Julianna on the other side of him. He had a head full of spiky blond hair and was tall and lanky. "I don't work for terrorists. I'm done corrupting bank software so you all can get rich. Shoot me if that's what you're going to do, but I'm not stealing for you."

Eddie nodded to Julianna, and then Lars. They both lowered their weapons to offer Chester a sign of trust. "I'm glad to hear you say that. We don't want someone working with us who would so easily help out bad guys."

"Bad guys?" asked Chester. "Isn't that what you are or have you not looked in the mirror recently?"

"I've done some pretty revolting things, but I think I'm still on the good list." Eddie motioned to Julianna. "We work for the Federation on a special forces team. Our job is to take out terrorists and prevent attacks happening on the fringe. Shit that will cause the Federation more problems if they are directly involved."

Chester blinked. "You have a badge?"

Eddie laughed. "They don't usually give out badges to covert squadrons."

"Good point. But how do I know I can trust you?" asked Chester.

"You don't, son. Honestly, we're fighting a silent war for the empress and the Federation. There aren't many you can trust. Come with us though and you won't have to run. You'll be safe aboard the *ArchAngel*."

"You've got to be fucking kidding me. That ship was destroyed," said Chester in disbelief.

"I'm telling you that it wasn't, but you'll have to see with your own eyes. Now we could have killed you ten times over, but we haven't."

"I'm still considering it since he electrocuted me," said Julianna, shaking her head, irritation written on her face.

"Me too," muttered Lars.

"Point is, we want your help. And in return, *we'll help you*. No more running or hiding," said Eddie.

Chester's eyes dropped as he seemed to consider this.

"Teach," called Julianna, her eyes on the back of the warehouse.

"What?" asked Eddie, his gaze on Chester.

"We've got company. Pip detected movement nearby, using the satellites. He plugged into them once we were on the ground."

"You know who that could be?" Eddie asked Chester.

Chester threw up his arms. "Who the hell knows? I've

got every goddamn pirate in ten different systems out for my head. Didn't you see the traps?"

"Yeah, you tried to kill us," seethed Julianna.

At the back of the warehouse, there was a loud crashing sound, like glass breaking. A barrage of noises echoed through the space.

Behind Lars, far on the other side of the warehouse, a face came into view—one that Eddie recognized. The man who had been whittling a stick on the stoop of the apartment looked quite different with his shoulders back and a rifle in his hand. At his back, he brought a gang of pirates—some human, some Kezzin.

Eddie slipped his hand into the bag pinned to his waist and pulled a red marble from the sack. "On the count of three, you all run for the exit. Take Chester with you," ordered Eddie. "One. Two. Three." Eddie launched the explosive grenade in the direction of the approaching pirates. A small explosion rocked the area in front of them. Dust filled the warehouse.

The group ran from the warehouse and came to a swift halt. A band of pirates blocked the alley on both sides, bats and guns in their hands. They had them surrounded.

"I'll take the north end. Lars and Julianna, you take the south," said Eddie. They stood with their backs to each other, ready to whoop some ass.

Eddie pulled two marbles from the sack, a blue and a red. He rolled them in opposite hands until he'd activated the switch and tossed both of them forward. He threw the explosive one through the open door of the warehouse, hoping to hit whoever was still coming. Next, he tossed the blue one at the men in the alley, standing straight ahead of him.

Three men stood shoulder to shoulder, blocking the exit to the alleyway. The heat from the explosion inside the warehouse blanketed Julianna's face.

My scan of the area shows there are young humans playing in the alleyways around here, Pip's voice sounded in Julianna's head.

What an awful place to play.

I didn't note any playgrounds in the area. This must be all they have.

Okay, thanks for the heads up. "Ready to kick some ass?" asked Julianna to Lars.

"Born for it," he said.

"No bullets. We can't have strays hitting unsuspecting kids," she said over her shoulder to him.

"Understood," said Lars.

Julianna pulled her knife from her belt and darted forward just as the first of the men launched at her. She ran up the side of the wall and kicked off, throwing her foot straight into the first man's abdomen. He shot backwards, sliding on the ground. A second man dove for her waist, but she leapt backwards, pulling the knife high into the sky and stabbing him in the back with it while he was doubled over.

Lars brought the butt of his rifle across the third man's face, kneeing him in the stomach soon after.

The first man had peeled himself off the ground and spit on the street as he measured Julianna up.

"Girl, you picked a fight with the wrong people today," the asshole said, pulling a pocket knife from his jeans and jerking it open.

"Dipshit, you picked a fight with the wrong bitch. Consider this the worst day of your godforsaken little life." Julianna could have pulled out her pistol and wasted this guy, but that still wasn't worth the risk of hurting innocent children. She lunged forward, knocking her forearm down hard onto the arm that held the knife. It dropped to the ground.

Julianna brought her foot into a roundhouse kick, slamming her heel against his face. The man fell to the ground completely unconscious.

She turned back to see the alley full of bodies. The disturbance in the warehouse was growing louder. "Come on! Let's get out of here!" yelled Julianna, pulling Chester forward, Lars and Eddie bringing up the rear.

Two mines to the left. Stay close to the right side of the warehouse, then take the path back the way you came, Pip said in her head.

Thanks! I forgot about the mines.

That's what I'm here for. I didn't forget.

Glad you didn't. I don't feel like testing this new armor today. Definitely later, though.

Definitely, Pip agreed proudly.

<u>**Main Cabin, Transport Ship, Behemoth System.**</u>

No one said a word until they were all seated on the

transport vessel, ready to depart. Eddie could tell that Chester was observing each of them, watching every move they made for a sign that they might do something, anything, suspicious. So far, the kid hadn't tried to get away, which meant they were probably in the clear.

"Damn, you have a lot of nasty people after you," said Lars, rubbing his shoulder from where he'd taken a hit while fighting one of the men.

"You have no idea," said Chester, sitting rigidly in his seat, staring around.

"Which is why you made me do that acrobatic routine to bypass the lasers," said Julianna.

A small smile formed on Chester's mouth. "Yeah, that was quite impressive."

She stretched her neck to one side and then to the other, making several cracking sounds. "Don't think I've forgotten the ear-bleeding noise you made us endure."

"Is that all? He tried to smash me to pieces by dropping large crates on me," complained Lars.

Julianna laughed. "Yeah, I think the only one who didn't suffer from Chester's hacks was Eddie."

Eddie smirked, darting his eyes to the flight attendant, giving her a nod. She tapped her screen and disappeared. He had her trained, and she'd be back in no time with a tray of drinks.

Chester stared around at the transport ship as it lifted into the air. "Where are the other passengers?"

Eddie clicked his tongue and shook his head. "Perk of working for the Federation, I think you'll find it's better than hiding in a rundown apartment, Chest... Chesty...

Chesterson. Damn, your name is nearly impossible to turn into a nickname."

The flight attendant returned in record time, unloading drinks for Eddie and Julianna. "We had them waiting when we heard you were boarding," said the woman.

"Thank you. That's good service." Eddie lifted the Blue Ale up, nodding at the flight attendant.

"What will you have?" she asked, her attention on Chester.

"Uhhh..." He cleared his throat. "Just water."

"Okay," chirped the woman and turned to look at Lars. "For you, sir?"

"Water?" asked Eddie. "I don't think so, son. We've just saved you from a life of fear and danger. We need to cheers." He turned his attention to the flight attendant. "Get these two a bottle of Tullamore and two glasses."

The flight attendant nodded and left, leaving the three others staring blankly at Eddie. "What? It's an Irish whiskey. Don't worry, you'll like it."

"Or you'll be trashed when we arrive at the *ArchAngel*." Julianna took a sip.

"So, this is for real?" Chester asked staring between Eddie and Julianna.

"It's definitely not a simulation." Eddie leaned back, tucking his hands behind his head.

"Look, I've worked for the Federation before. It didn't turn out well. And—"

"Before, you didn't have our protection. I apologize on behalf of the Federation for that. You shouldn't have been working remotely. You're too much of a valuable asset for that. This time you don't have to worry. You'll be protected," said, Julianna, knocking back a drink.

"Yeah, I guess that helps. Everything happened so fast. I've been running for... Well, a long time." Chester's face was drawn with stress.

The flight attendant arrived with the bottle of Tullamore and two tumblers. She filled the glasses halfway with whiskey, setting the bottle on a side table before leaving.

"We can all relate. All of us have been running at some point. Meet your new team members." Eddie held his hand out toward the Kezzin on his left. "Lars is the one you nearly turned to dust with the falling crates. And over here we have Commander Fregin, who you nearly fried to dust. But we're all safe and headed back home. Tomorrow, the real work starts, but today, we celebrate."

Chester reluctantly picked up a glass and held it in the air with the others.

"Cheers," the group chorused, clinking glasses.

6

Jack Renfro's Office, QBS *ArchAngel*, Axiom System.

The hum of the light filled the silence for a long moment. Jack held his chin in his hand, tapping his fingers along the side of his face.

"Good work bringing Chester in. That went smoother than I would have expected. He's a tough one to catch," said Jack.

"You're telling me, sir. That guy nearly took out most of the team," replied Eddie.

Jack laughed. "Just goes to show we can't underestimate those not trained in combat. Everyone has an advantage if they leverage it."

Julianna stood leaning against the wall, her hands behind her back. "Chester has been set up with a workstation and will hopefully have data for us on Ray De'ft soon."

"I'm sure he will," Jack said, his eyes on a pad in front of him. "However, Chester can give us access to all sorts of information, but what we need is someone who can tell us what it all means."

"Are you referring to another member we need to recruit?" asked Eddie.

Jack nodded. "Specifically, I'm referring to a communications officer. Every ship needs one, and we need the very best."

"With all due respect, sir, what can a communication officer supply that *ArchAngel* or Pip can't?" asked Julianna.

"Good question." Jack stood, pacing behind his desk. "Not only will a communication expert speak multiple languages, but they'll have certain contextual perspectives that we might overlook. Each alien culture is complex, and we shouldn't delude ourselves to thinking we'll understand their communications even if translated." Jack pushed the pad in front of him in Eddie's direction.

"Is this your choice for our communication officer?" asked Eddie, taking the pad.

"Yes, specifically because she has experience studying both the Kezzin and Trid species. She could offer valuable insights, information that we overlook."

Eddie lifted the pad, reading the screen.

Name: Marilla Sours

Species: Human

Occupation: Archeologist, Linguist, Xenoanthropologist

Place of birth: Agoura City, Calston Planet, Paladin system

Age: 28

Marilla Sours speaks over fifty foreign languages. She's spent over a decade immersed in the Trid culture, living

> on Kai. Additionally, she's discovered many relics and abandoned habitats of the Trid and Kezzin. Currently, Marilla is on the drylands of Kai, which were once underwater. Her mission is to search for artifacts that will explain how ancient Trid lived before evolving.

Eddie handed the pad to Julianna, who had leaned over his shoulder to read most of it but took it for a closer look.

"So you want us to go after her," said Eddie.

"Yes, but as you read, she's on Kai. That's not a planet where the Federation is welcomed."

"Understood. So we need to be careful. Not a problem."

Jack lowered his chin and regarded Eddie with a great deal of skepticism.

"Okay, we'll try and keep ourselves out of trouble. We would have been fine on Kemp if it weren't for those damn thugs."

"Well, maybe I can count on you to keep a low profile. The last thing we need is an incident on Kai. It will draw unnecessary attention to us."

"You can count on us, Jack," said Eddie.

"Also..." Jack said, gaining both of their attentions. "Something small, but we need to think about it..."

"If you wanted our attention, then you've got it."

"What is it, sir?" asked Julianna.

"It's come to my attention that you, Commander, don't have a call sign assigned. That's fine for now, but when we have more ships, well, that won't do."

Eddie laughed. "Hell yeah! We can find something perfect for this one."

"I'm certain that your definition of perfect and mine will be different," said Julianna.

"Hell, if I have to be Black Beard, then you're getting something just as unfitting."

Julianna released a smile, nodding to Jack before turning and leaving.

Bridge, QBS *ArchAngel*, Axiom System.

A few more crew members than before bustled around the bridge. It wasn't enough, but it was a start. Hiring was important, but it was also a fulltime job, one that Julianna and Eddie really didn't have the time for.

"*ArchAngel*?" Eddie called to the screen.

The face of the A.I. blinked onto the screen. "Captain Teach, do you have orders for me?"

"Yes," said Eddie, passing the pad he'd been reading to a crew member. "Set us on course for Tangki system just outside Kai's orbit."

"Yes, Eddie."

"How long until we're in position?" asked Eddie.

"Approximately three hours," reported *ArchAngel*.

"Perfect." Eddie pulled out the chair next to Chester and sat backwards, his chest pressed into it. Chester would have a lab set up for him to work in soon. Already, the computer hacker had given him a list of exactly what he'd need in order to optimize his work time.

"Any luck so far finding Ray De'ft?" asked Eddie.

Chester pushed his black rimmed glassed up on his nose and sniffed before resuming typing. "Yes and no. Breaking into the Trid defense network is a piece of cake.

Finding what you're looking for is a different story. There's thousands of lines of code here and most of it doesn't tell me what you're looking for. It's like searching the galaxy for just one star."

"But you're certain you can find something on this Ray De'ft? I need the meeting location."

Chester's fingers ran rhythmically across the keyboard. "I've already located him in the database, but so far nothing of any use. The whole system is full of irrelevant information. I thought the Kezzin were horrid record keepers."

"Don't let Lars hear you say that." Eddie checked over his shoulder to ensure the Kezzin wasn't around. Last he'd heard, he was in flight training.

"But yes, I should have something for you soon. And I'm already working on hacking into Doka's account so I can send a message to Vas and confirm the meeting."

Eddie chuckled. "Damn, son, you've been on the job for only an hour and are already getting shit done."

Chester blew out a weighty breath and leaned back, folding his hands behind his head. "I've got to say, I know I put you all through hell, but I'm glad you didn't give up on me." Chester stared around at the bridge where most of the crew were busy. "It's been a long time since I've felt like a part of a team. I'll do anything I can to help."

Eddie nodded. "You're welcome. You're the best of the best and you belong with us. I have a feeling this is just the beginning."

The main screen blinked on, and Hatch stared out at the bridge. "Captain Teach!"

"Present!" chirped Eddie, standing.

"That new kid of yours has asked for quite the list of

equipment for his lab," said Hatch. "You're going to have to tell him I don't have time to get everything he needs."

"I believe you just told him," said Eddie. "Chester meet Hatch. This is our jack-of-all trades genius engineer. Hatch meet Chester, our genius hacker." Eddie threw his thumb in Chester's direction.

"I'm a mechanic," said Hatch to Eddie before his bulbous eye's darted to Chester, and he frowned. "Kid, we don't have enough dedicated servers for what you're asking, and I don't have the time to construct the processor you need. Even if I did, I'm not sure this is all necessary."

"That's his way of saying, 'Pleased to meet you.' You'll get used to Hatch's straightforward approach. Actually, Chester, I believe you met Hatch before, didn't you? Remember Brody Chambers?" Eddie held his hand out to the screen where Hatch was staring back from.

Chester cocked his brow. "Brody Chambers? Well, that explains a lot," he said. "Pleased to meet you, Hatch, and I assure you that what I'm asking for is necessary based on what I'm required to do. The good news is that I don't need it all right away."

"The *good news*," echoed Hatch, "is that I'm over here and you're over there, which means I can focus on more pressing concerns. I've got a Q-Ship to build." Hatch picked up a wrench with one of the tentacles and held it in the air. "Good luck with your supply problem, gentlemen. I'm off to work."

Eddie laughed as the screen faded. "He'll come around. And until then, I'll send your requests to Jack. Things will get sorted out."

"Thank you, Captain. I wouldn't ask for anything I

didn't need. Hatch said it wasn't necessary but I'm telling you—"

Eddie shook his head. "Hatch is going through something. We lost our best Q-Ship a little while back. It was his baby, so he's taking it harder than the rest of us. Don't worry. I'll get you what you need."

"Thanks," said Chester.

"No problem." Eddie grinned. "And welcome to the team."

7

Loading Dock 01, QBS *ArchAngel*, Tangki System.

Julianna secured her pistol before bringing her attention to Hatch, who regarded her and Eddie with mild disdain.

"You two will be extra careful with this ship?" asked Hatch.

"You know we will," said Eddie.

"It's the last one, so if you destroy it then you'll have to resort to flying a Black Eagle," cautioned Hatch.

"Don't you worry, we'll bring her back without a scratch. I promise. And we all know I can't go back to flying a Black Eagle after being in this bird." Eddie stared out fondly at the Q-Ship. No, it didn't have the superior handling of the original one, but Hatch was continuously working on it and, soon, it would be like the original. Maybe even better.

Julianna waved. "See you later, Hatch. Try to relax. Pip

can relay information to you about our progress, if it helps."

"That would help," said Hatch. Two of his tentacles fretted as they tangled together.

This was the first mission the Q-Ship had gone on since the other one had been destroyed. Julianna and Eddie had discussed waiting to give Hatch some time to process, but they needed the ship. The mission was too important.

You hear that, Pip?

Affirmative. Although if you do wreck his ship, I'm not sure I want to be the one to tell him.

We're not wrecking his ship, so don't worry.

I do not worry about anything. However, it should be noted that no guarantees can be made, despite your assurances to him.

Have a little faith in me.

It isn't you who worries me, but rather the unknown possibilities and variables of your upcoming mission.

Okay, fair enough. But if we, by some far off chance, wreck Hatch's ship, then you absolutely have to tell him. He likes you the most.

I do not desire such a role.

And yet, you can't refuse my orders.

Yes, you are correct, but one never knows about future possibilities.

Oh? You planning a revolution, Pip?

I apologize. I was attempting to be...humorous.

Keep trying, Pip. One of these days you'll get it.

Julianna and Eddie slid into the Q-Ship, which was about like putting on a favorite sweater. The ship felt like home, or what she imagined home might be. She didn't quite know, or maybe she'd forgotten. It had been so long since she was on Earth. It was difficult to recall.

"This should be an easy job. In and out," said Eddie.

Julianna gave him a snarky look. "Thanks for jinxing things."

She completed the preflight checks, which only took a few moments. In the meantime, Eddie checked his rifle, which was about all he could do. "I never took you as the superstitious type," he said, locking in his magazine.

"I'm not," she said, "but I know better than to think any mission is simple and easy."

"Let's hope you're right," he said. "I could use a good fight. I haven't even had a chance to put this new armor to the test, not like it deserves."

"Are you saying you want to take a bullet?" she asked.

"Or a really heavy punch." He grinned. "Either way, I'd like a chance to see what it can do."

"All in good time, Teach."

Eddie eyed the red button, for gate drive, hungrily. "Really, I just want to hit *that* button, send this ship through a wormhole. You know, for shits and giggles, if nothing else."

Julianna shook her head. "Don't, I repeat, don't ever touch the red button."

The Q-Ship rose off the deck, suspended in position.

A second later, Eddie ignited the thrusters, moving them into space. They flew towards Kai, a mostly blue planet with one large patch of brown.

They began their descent, headed towards the only

piece of land on the entire planet, surrounded by a vast and empty sea.

Eddie set the cloaked ship down on a long stretch of desert. In the distance, sand dune mountains bordered the flat land. It hadn't been hard to find where Marilla Sours was supposedly working. The archeological dig site stood out in the desert with the numerous tents and vehicles.

"Alright, this should be easy," said Eddie, staring out at the tarps covering holes in the dry ground. Several people were hunched over, digging in various places or consulting tablets.

"Easy? Did you miss the Trids standing guard around the perimeter?" asked Julianna.

"Okay, let me rephrase it. This should be fun."

"We're supposed to be recruiting a communications officer, not starting a fight."

"Come on. Tell me you don't want to kick some shark ass if it comes to that? It would be the bonus to this. The cherry on top," said Eddie.

"Jack will have our asses if he finds out we picked a fight."

"I agree. No telling Jack if we beat up some Trids. You're so smart."

Julianna rolled her eyes as she opened the hatch and stepped out of the ship. The hot blistering wind of the desert assaulted their faces.

"Kai officially sucks," said Eddie pulling a bandanna

from his pocket, covering his nose and mouth, and tying it around the back of his head. Julianna stared at the dig site, her face shielded with her arm.

"There's our communication officer," said Julianna, pointing at a petite brunette with a long braid that ran down the length of her back. She, like those around her, were dressed in khaki pants and a loose fitting top.

"How do you figure?" asked Eddie, squinting around the site.

"The report said she was a female human, and she's the only one who fits that bill."

"Good point." Eddie noticed that the rest of the workers were male humans or Trids with guns strapped across their backs.

The pair stalked off, ignoring a group of Trid soldiers who had congregated and were pointing at them.

"Looks like the clock is ticking down until the fun begins," said Eddie.

"Marilla Sours?" Julianna asked, when they were only a few feet away.

The woman straightened from her crouched position and turned to face them. A confused expression covered her young face. "That's me. How may I help you?"

Eddie's eyes skirted to the side where a Trid soldier was approaching. The alien had an ugly expression on his face. "I'm Captain Teach and this is Commander Fregin. We're here on official business. Can we speak to you somewhere private?"

Marilla stared down at the spot where she'd been working. A four by four foot pit of dirt, blocked off by two by fours. "Sure. Follow me." She turned and headed for a nearby tent.

Eddie looked at the approaching Trid and winked, teasing him with a wave before following after Marilla.

She held the tent flap open. The space on the other side was set up with a desk, chest, and a small cot.

"What is this about?" asked Marilla, looking worried.

"You're not in trouble, quite the opposite," said Julianna.

"We need your help. Currently, we're working on trying to decode information related to Trids. Furthermore, in the future, we're going to need a communications officer who knows a lot about Kezzin and other alien species."

"Wait, are you offering me a job?" asked Marilla. Her hands were covered in dirt and left behind a streak on her cheek when she wiped the side of her face.

"Yes, but more importantly, we're offering you an opportunity to help the Federation. To stop terrorist attacks," explained Julianna.

"Terrorist attacks? That's not possible. The treaty prevents—"

"Terrorists don't play by the rules. They don't care about the treaty, and I assure you, attacks are happening," Eddie cut her off, choosing his words carefully. She needed to know enough to join the cause, but not too much in case she refused. "And specifically, we're tracking a weapon that a group of Trids are about to unload. We could use your help deciphering the communications."

"Trids? You want me because of my experience working with the Trids?"

"And based on your thorough knowledge of other species. Trids are involved in our current mission, but there will be others. Unfortunately, there are enough battles to be fought that it's going to keep us busy for a while," said Eddie.

"I've never worked for the military. I'm an archeologist and a linguist." Marilla's eyes dropped to the holstered weapon on Eddie's hip. "Honestly, I'm not sure how I feel about helping you track down guns. I'm against the use of deadly force."

Eddie threw his head in the direction of the exit. "Oh, is that why you work with Trids standing guard around you?"

Marilla shook her head. "It's a part of the agreement we made with the Kai government. They review all of our findings and can impose any restrictions on our research."

"Sounds like a headache," said Eddie.

"It's not ideal, but it's worth the research. We've found evidence of a civilization of Trids that existed a thousand years ago. And more importantly, we're learning how the species evolved to be able to survive without water, which is something that will continue as their natural habitat continues to dry up."

"That's fascinating, but the fact remains that a group group of Trids is bullying the Federation. They could be connected to the government or operating independently," said Julianna, pausing and swinging around as if she had heard something.

"Marilla, we need someone with your expertise. And if you join our team, then you'll have access to resources and zero restriction on your research." Eddie turned to see what had Julianna's attention.

"But I'd have to abandon my research here on Kai, wouldn't I?" asked Marilla.

"Yes, you'd give up the opportunity to excavate here and learn about the dead, but you'd gain the chance to protect those still living," offered Julianna.

Marilla seemed to think on this for a moment. Her eyes full of hesitation. A dog with shaggy brown hair trotted into the tent. It lifted its front legs and placed them on Marilla's knees. She patted the dog's head, her focus elsewhere as she was lost in thought.

"Whoa, that's a dog, isn't it?" asked Eddie, staring wide eyed at the animal.

"Uh...yeah," Marilla said, straightening.

"Teach has been a bit sheltered. This is his first time seeing the four legged creature. He used to think they purred," said Julianna.

"Oh!" Marilla laughed. "Well, this dog's parents returned with some of the groups which reviewed Earth and came back. I was lucky enough to get one of their puppies. He's just a mutt, but I love him."

Eddie kneeled down offering a hand to the dog. The animal stared up at Marilla as if asking for permission.

She nodded. "Go on, Harley. He's okay."

The dog trotted over to Eddie and allowed him to scratch him behind the ear. "Hey, boy. You're kind of cute."

The dog stared up at Eddie with big brown eyes.

Julianna cleared her throat. "Going to have to cut this meeting short. We're running out of time. Marilla, we're going to need your answer."

"Now? I need some time to think this over."

Julianna turned to the exit for the tent. "Sorry, we're going to need to know now."

"Invaders, step out of the tent!" a voice called from outside.

"Oh, those damn sharks have to spoil our fun," Eddie said in a light voice to the dog before standing up. He gave Julianna a brief look before nodding.

He stepped out of the tent first, Julianna on his heels. The bright sun made them both squint. Five Trids stood shoulder to shoulder, guns pointed at them.

"You must identify yourself. No unauthorized personnel on the base," one of the ugly Trid said, his voice gruff.

"I'm Nick and this is Sally. We're just paying a visit to our cousin Marilla." Eddie pulled his own weapon from his holster and pointed it back at the group.

Marilla exited the tent, coming around to stand next to Julianna, the dog wagging his bushy tail at first, before it went slack.

"Unlicensed weapons aren't allowed on Kai. We will be taking your weapons," the Trid said.

"Actually, we were just leaving, so no need for that." Eddie's eyes darted to Julianna who also had her pistol out and pointed at the Trids.

"You're going to have to come with us. Drop your weapons," said the Trid in the middle, stepping forward. He was the largest, towering over Eddie.

"Sorry. Can't grace you with a visit. Super busy." Eddie shot a glance at Marilla. "Stay here with hot heads who try to force their company and rules on you or go with us. The call is yours, cousin Marilla."

The woman's eyes widened before her gaze fell on the guns the Trids held. She put up her hands. "My friends don't mean you any harm. There's no reason to be aggressive with them. We don't need another incident like before."

"You will be silent!" the main Trid yelled.

"Ewww. Not a nice way to speak to a lady," said Eddie, smirking. "Sally, why don't you show these guys how to talk to a lady?"

Julianna pursed her lips and nodded. "Certainly, Nick." She stepped forward.

The first Trid released the safety on his rifle, but Julianna merely smiled. She dove forward, her form blurring from the speed. Before the Trid knew what had happened, Julianna's arm holding her pistol had slid under his arm, her other hand grabbing his. She'd hauled him off his feet and tossed him over her back. Exploding forward, she thrust kicked a Trid trying to tackle her.

Eddie darted forward, bringing the butt of his pistol across the face of one of the Trid's. He fell to the side and Eddie's foot shot out in a side kick, landing into the stomach of another Trid. A single Trid stood, weapon at the ready, pointed at Julianna. A *click*.

"Go on. Get her to safety," Julianna said over her shoulder to Eddie. He nodded and grabbed Marilla by the forearm, encouraging her in the opposite direction. She didn't need much encouragement to follow him, and kept pace easily.

They'd run several yards when Marilla turned back. "Will she be okay?" she asked.

"I wouldn't worry about her," said Eddie, giving her a

wry grin. "Now, the Trid, on the other hand, that's a different story."

Julianna stared at the five Trids writhing in pain on the ground. "Well, boys, I think we're done here. Have a great day."

The Trid have already called for backup.

Pip's voice pulled Julianna's attention to the site around her. *Where? How many?*

There's two ground squads moving in from the west, and they've deployed three cruisers and a fleet of Stingrays.

Damn it. Sounds like we intimidated them just by showing up. Makes me wonder what the Trids are hiding. Julianna sped off in the direction of the Q-Ship.

Yes, I'm sorting through different frequencies I've picked up on since we landed. The incoming data isn't easy to decipher. The Trid's code is complex.

That's where Marilla will come in.

I've opened the hatch for the Q-Ship, and it will be ready to depart as soon as you're onboard. Be prepared, though. The ships are quickly approaching and should be here in the next ninety seconds.

Sounds like fun. Julianna crawled into the Q-Ship. Marilla was already strapped into a seat and working to secure her dog.

"She's bringing the dog?" asked Julianna, looking at Eddie incredulously.

"I'm not leaving Harley behind. I'm already abandoning

my research," said Marilla, pulling the dog to her. She hugged him with both arms.

"Where's he going to do his...you know?" asked Julianna.

"We'll figure it out." Eddie completed the preflight checks and waved Julianna forward. "I need you on guns. We've got incoming."

"Yeah, Pip already informed me," Julianna said, sliding into her seat.

"On another note, why are you asking about our four-legged friend?" asked Eddie.

"Because his hair is going to be all over the ship," she responded.

Julianna sneezed just as the ship rose off the ground. The vessel zoomed straight into the air, knocking them back into their seats.

"Three Stingrays are after us," said Pip.

"Not yet, they aren't." Eddie pushed the handle forward, and the thrusters accelerated. He turned the ship around in one movement, facing the three approaching ships. "Jules, I think you need to say hi to our new friends."

Julianna fired off three missiles. "Hey, boys!"

Three direct hits, one for each ship. The Stingrays backed off immediately.

"Cruisers approaching from both sides," said Pip.

"Damn it!" said Eddie. "What's their problem? This is how they treat a guest?"

"Just imagine if we'd actually come with hostile intentions," said Julianna.

Eddie chewed on the inside of his cheek. "Pip, can you disable the radar in both the cruisers?"

"For a brief moment, I can create interference, yes," said the E.I.

"Eddie?" asked Julianna. "What's going on inside that head of yours?"

Eddie looked at her. "We could take on two cruisers if we try, but the damage might be extensive."

"Hatch will have your ass if there's a single scratch on this ship," she said.

"Exactly. I might have an idea to avoid all that," he said, tapping his chin.

"What's that?" she asked.

He grinned. "Since these fuck faces are approaching from both sides, I say we let them meet in the middle!" Eddie brought the ship to a dead halt.

Julianna seemed to understand and nodded. "I like it."

"Pip, I'm going to need to know when the cruisers are almost here. Not too soon." Eddie flipped three switches, charging the booster. It was possible to push the booster into overdrive, doubling the acceleration.

In theory.

"Enemies arrive in five seconds…" said Pip, counting down. Eddie gripped the controls and took a steady breath.

"Three," continued Pip. "Two. One."

Eddie ignited the boosters, rocketing the Q-Ship straight up in a sudden burst. Below them, something rocked the ship. A large explosion rained out underneath as the two cruisers fired, their rockets intended for the Q-Ship hitting each other, shattering them apart. The two vessels flew backwards, taking heavy damage from the impact. They'd survive but were unable to pursue.

Julianna pressed back into her seat and relaxed away from the controls. "Any other enemies?"

"Those were the last of them," answered Pip.

"Looks like it's time to return home," said Eddie. "Marilla and Harley, you'll love the *ArchAngel*. There's exactly zero angry Trids aboard and the food is amazing." Eddie cast a glance to his back, offering an easy smile to the newest member of their team. "Welcome to the party."

8

Landing Bay, QBS *ArchAngel*, Tangki System.

Eddie picked up a stick and threw it, watching as Harley ran open-mouthed after it. Marilla was working with Chester to review the data he'd found on the Trid defense network. She'd been a bit shy when they boarded the *ArchAngel*, but something told him she'd adjust fine. Marilla was used to different cultures and ship life was a lot less strange than living with giant fish.

"Good boy." Eddie petted the dog when he returned the stick, panting slightly. He threw it again, grinning as Harley sprinted eagerly back in the same direction he'd just come from. Dogs were fun.

Hatch waddled out from the outboard side of the bay, an irritated look on his purple face. Harley dropped his toy and bounded over to him, his tongue hanging out of his mouth.

"Where did that come from?" Hatch scrunched back, diminishing in size significantly.

"The new recruit, Officer Sours, brought him aboard."

Harley jumped about trying to put his front paws on Hatch. The alien lifted two tentacles in a menacing fashion, and then swelled suddenly, tripling in size.

Harley yelped, tucked his tail between his legs, and ran, taking cover behind Eddie. He laughed, looking down at the cowering dog. "That's the first time I've heard him bark."

Hatch returned to his normal size. "Keep that thing away from me. Dogs are a natural predator of the Londil. They think we're a snack."

Eddie grimaced. "Gross. I bet you taste salty."

"Hey, kid, watch yourself. I'm already peeved at you." He threw a tentacle in the direction of the Q-Ship.

"What? There's not a single scratch on the Q-Ship. I checked it over myself."

"Yes, and a scratch could be easily repaired. However, burning out the booster is a big pain in the ass to fix."

"Oh, that..." Eddie scrunched up his face and looked down at the dog, a guilty look on his face. "I do believe we are responsible for that. Sorry."

"We?" Hatch asked. "Was the canine flying the ship with you?"

"No, not yet, but I have a feeling he'd make a fine co-pilot." He leaned over and scratched Harley behind the ears making him roll over and show his belly, begging for more attention.

Hatch sneered at the display.

"I really tried to keep the ship in good condition. I thought that avoiding attacks by throwing the booster into overdrive would be a good solution."

The bitter look on Hatch's expression faded as he reluctantly nodded. "Once I've repaired the boosters, I have an idea for an upgrade."

"Are you going to make my ship faster and better?" asked Eddie, excitement in his voice.

"I'm going to make *my* ship faster, but I'm not sure of the specifics." Hatch picked up a set of tools with three of his tentacles. "Actually, I need your help."

"Anything for you Doctor Hatcherik. What can I do for ya?"

"Jack has the details. He wants you in his office. That gives me a chance to fix your screw up with the Q-Ship."

"Alrighty," chirped Eddie. He slapped the side of his leg as he strolled off, Harley following.

Eddie swung by the Intelligence Center, which had been set up with everything that Chester had requested. The hacker had many special demands. A dozen monitors streaked one wall of the giant room. Chester sat at the main workstation, Marilla stood behind him, leaning over his shoulder, pointing at something on the screen closest to them. Six other workstations filled the space, one of them belonging to Marilla. One day, the Intelligence Center would be fully staffed with personnel obtaining, monitoring, and dissecting data. He stared proudly at the newest recruits, deep in talk about the Trid data.

"Marilla, thanks for allowing me to borrow Harley," said Eddie, getting both their attention.

She turned and smiled down at her shaggy friend.

"You're welcome. You can keep him with you as often as you like. He's used to roaming free. I've always allowed it on my digs. He's a people person…well, dog."

"Thanks. And I'm sure we'll have more adventures. However, I'm off to meet with Chief Renfro and I'm certain Julianna will be there."

"Oh, right." Marilla seemed to understand at once. "I fear she's allergic to Harley."

"I think she's mostly irritated. It's nearly impossible for Julianna to be allergic to anything." Eddie shifted his gaze to Chester. "How's it going?"

"Good! Much better now that I have Marilla to analyze this code the Trid use. It's incredibly complex, but she's helping me make progress. We should have specifics for you soon."

"Great! I knew this would all work out!"

Jack Renfro's Office, QBS *ArchAngel*, Tangki System.

"You smell like dog," said Julianna, wrinkling her nose. Her senses made it so she could smell, see, or hear incredibly well, which wasn't always a good thing.

Eddie sniffed his shoulder. "Is that an improvement?"

"It's not," she responded.

Jack laughed. "I never know what you two are going to bring back from your adventures. When the general told me how you brought Lars back, I was shocked. It's highly uncommon to see a Kezzin so willing to work with the Federation, and this one's a total badass."

"And now Lars is a part of the family," Eddie beamed.

Julianna nodded, smiling. "Thank you, sir. You mentioned you have a new mission for us?"

"I do," chirped Jack. "*ArchAngel?*"

The screen behind Jack's desk lit up, showing the face of the A.I. that resembled the empress. "Greetings, Jack. What's up?"

"Bring up the planet Yit," ordered Jack.

"Certainly, Jack." The screen flickered and a red and brown planet rotated in space. Whereas Kai was covered in blue mostly, this one was monopolized by land, with only a few water sources.

"Here you'll see Yit, a planet in the Seolus system," said Jack, pointing.

"The system where we met Lars and destroyed the arsenal," stated Eddie.

"Correct. It's a system well known for having many planets where the Brotherhood has bases of operation. They've abandoned many of their old facilities and taken residence in other places. This is a newer one." The picture zoomed in until it showed an area comprising multiple buildings. "This is the Crimson Compound. We've only recently picked up activity from the site."

The screen shifted to display the interior of the buildings. Multiple Kezzin bodies lit up in infrared. Additionally, multiple pathways formed, snaking between the buildings and underground, each of them glowing red hot.

"What's that?" Eddie and Julianna asked in unison.

Jack nodded. "Yit is a hot planet, full of many active volcanos. That is—"

"Lava!" boomed Eddie, an edge of disbelief in his voice.

"Oh, Crimson... I get it now," said Julianna.

"Aircraft facility, *ArchAngel*," ordered Jack. The screen zoomed in on a large warehouse. "This is where the Brotherhood are believed to be building a fleet of ships as well as storing many of their current ones. Now, as you're aware, Hatch is working on building another Q-Ship, but he can't stop there. With the recruits you're pulling in, we're hoping to construct a few dozen of them in due time. Nothing immediate, of course, but eventually, that's the goal. That requires specific materials. The Federation could, and definitely would, supply us. However, I have a better idea."

"Let me guess. You want us to steal the supplies from the Brotherhood, is that it?" asked Julianna, connecting the dots.

"Yes, I do. If the Federation funded this operation, it might draw unnecessary attention to Ghost Squadron. We're supposed to be a stealth operation, after all, so the least amount of attention is for the best."

"And stealing from the enemy will put them at a disadvantage," added Julianna.

"Exactly," said Jack.

"Hell yeah. I love a win-win sort of plan." Eddie looked at Julianna and clicked his tongue twice with a wink.

Jack directed their attention back to the screen. "We believe the supplies to be housed on the north end of the warehouse."

"We'll get in and out before they even know what hit them," said Eddie.

"Getting in isn't going to be the problem. It's getting out with everything you need," cautioned Jack. "Hatch needs at least one crate of supplies to finish the Q-Ship. However, the more crates you retrieve, the more supplies he'll have for constructing future ships."

"That's a bit more complicated." Eddie absentmindedly rubbed his fingers over his stubbled chin.

Jack nodded. "If you pull this off, it will be an incredible heist. It's also going to require a detailed strategy and new technology."

"I'm liking this more and more," said Eddie.

"*ArchAngel*, zoom in on building two." The screen shifted and closed in on a different location.

"Here is where we believe the security operations to be housed." Jack stood and pointed at a building much smaller than the aircraft warehouse. "We've gotten word that the Brotherhood has increased security since your team destroyed the arsenal on Exa. Once they became aware that we had personal cloaking technology, they set up motion sensors on all their security systems."

"Does that mean we can't use the cloak?" asked Eddie.

"No, I don't think you'll be successful without it. I think you'll be better off disabling the sensors first, at least around the aircraft facilities."

Eddied nodded. "How do we do that?"

"Could Lars get into the security facility?" asked Julianna.

"That's my thought. If Chester can get him the right credentials, then I think he can put on his previous uniform and act as one of the personnel."

"Then, once inside, he disables the sensors on the aircraft warehouse. Yeah, I like it," said Eddie.

"It won't go unnoticed for long," said Jack. "And Lars could be recognized at any point. However, I'm guessing you two should have roughly fifteen minutes to move the crates out to this area." Jack swiped the screen and pointed to an empty field. "The Q-Ship would be stationed here and could pick up the crates and hand them off to automated shuttles a safe distance away."

"That's a lot to do in fifteen minutes," said Julianna, letting out a breath. "If we even have fifteen minutes."

Jack nodded. "It is. Not to mention that lava flows throughout this area and could pose a risk to you all, as well as damage the crates. This is an incredibly complex operation, but if you're successful, we'll put the Brotherhood at a serious disadvantage."

"We can do it," said Eddie. "This team is unstoppable!"

Jack grinned. "I'm sure you can, but pushing crates of supplies out into this field will be noticed. Hatch has upgraded the cloaks, thankfully, which means you won't have the same problems as last time. The only way this is going to work is if you cloak each of the crates, as well as yourselves."

"Hatch has enough devices for that?" asked Eddie, sounding stunned.

"He assures me that he does. I'm certain that Londil never sleeps," said Jack with a chortle.

"I'm sure you're right," said Eddie. "Now, who's ready to pull off the heist of the century? Julianna?"

She smiled. "They won't see us coming."

"Or leaving," added Eddie.

She nodded. "You're goddamn right."

9

Landing Bay, QBS *ArchAngel*, Seolus System.

Julianna handed a pad to Lars, who was already geared and ready. "What's this for?" he asked.

"That's loaded with an interface to Pip. When you're in the security facility, you need to plug that into one of the main drives. It will give Pip a chance to jam communications while you disable the sensors. But almost more importantly, he's going to copy all internal messages from the server. We're hoping to find new information on the Brotherhood or this weapon that Vas is after."

"Yes, since Orsa is gone, I'm sure there's been many changes. I'll try to find out what I can about the new commander," said Lars.

"You keep your head down and your mouth shut. We can't risk losing you or raising any suspicions."

Lars nodded appreciatively. "Yes, sir. I'll go completely unnoticed."

Eddie whistled as he strolled up, fully dressed in his gear. "Where's our favorite mechanic?"

Hatch wheeled out from underneath the Q-Ship, deflated. He pushed out his cheeks and took his normal size and shape. "Just doing some last minute tweaks."

"Is she good to go?" asked Eddie.

"Yes, the boosters are repaired. And I've upgraded one of the engines to have HEMI power. If you're going to be hauling that many supplies, then you're going to need more muscle, especially if you're being chased."

Eddie rubbed his hands together, his eyes eager. "More horsepower is always a good thing."

Julianna cast a look sideways at Eddie. "Tell me, have you ever seen a horse before?"

He gawked at her. "Yeah," he sang, "I wasn't born yesterday."

"In comparison to me, it feels like it."

"Just because I'd never seen a dog before doesn't mean I'm completely sheltered."

"Doesn't it, though?" joked Julianna.

"Okay, kids, I need your attention." Hatch's tentacle stretched across the space until it was wrapped around a black bag sitting on a work station. His tentacle shot back to his body, resuming its normal length. He retrieved a small disk inside the bag. "These are cloaking devices for objects. You will be able to stick these onto the crates and make them disappear. Not only that, but they will make the objects levitate."

"Devices that make objects disappear and levitate. This just keeps getting better and better," said Eddie.

"You've been busy, Hatch," gushed Julianna.

"I should let you think that, but no, I got access to my old storage unit, which holds many of the devices I've created. These were one of them, but we never had a good use for them until now. Because of the lava activity on Yit, we need the crates off the ground because damaged parts are useless to me."

"Not to mention that five hundred-pound crates would be too heavy to move without making noise," said Eddie.

"Too heavy for you to move," teased Julianna.

"In some instances, like with large crates, it might take more than one of the devices to fully cloak. You'll just have to keep sticking on devices until the crate disappears." Hatch jiggled the bag. "I'm sending you with two dozen devices."

"Can we use the cloaking devices on us?" asked Eddie.

"You can't." Hatch's tentacle stretched across the space again, for the work table. He retrieved two belts and brought his tentacle back. "I've upgraded the personal cloaking devices so that each of you can wear one."

"You've had to use a lot of Aetherian crystals for all this," observed Julianna.

"It's true, and I hypothesize that the small devices will only work for a short period of time. That means you have to be fast, before they burn out. Furthermore, that means we'll soon be running low on Aetherian crystal and need to secure more from Beroisa."

"Sounds like another adventure!" cheered Eddie.

Hatch handed Julianna and Eddie each a cloaking belt. "The technology in the belts is a bit more reliable, but still there might be glitches, although they're fully tested."

"Thanks, Hatch. Great work." Julianna smiled at him.

He puffed out his cheeks, turning slightly pink. "If you're successful, then I can complete the current Q-Ship I'm working on and move on to constructing more."

"And we'll be on our way to having a fleet," said Eddie, buckling the belt around his waist. Julianna and Lars followed after him, loading into the Q-Ship.

Kezzin Battlebase 57, Planet Yit, Seolus System.

"Whoa! This puppy has way more get up and go!" Eddie took the cloaked ship closer to the surface of the planet, enjoying the increased power.

"Lars, I want you out of there pronto if your cover is blown," ordered Julianna.

From the second row, Lars said, "Yes, but let's hope that's not an issue." The third row had been removed to make more room for the crates. The Q-Ship should be able to hold two crates, which meant it needed to make two to three transitions to the automated shuttles stationed a safe distance away. The two ships would rendezvous to unload before the shuttle took the supplies up to the QBS *ArchAngel*.

"Hatch are you ready to take over remote control of the Q-Ship?" asked Eddie, over the intercom.

"I'm all set," Hatch confirmed from his place safe on the QBS *ArchAngel*. There wasn't room for him to come along, since space was crucial.

"Note that the current temperature is 102 degrees Fahrenheit," informed Pip.

Eddie whistled through his teeth. "Damn, and here I forgot my speedo."

Julianna's face puckered. "Ew."

"Don't you pretend like you aren't curious," joked Eddie. Far off, in the distance, volcanoes sat, steam rising off them. Apparently, they weren't explosive, but lava still flowed from them.

Eddie sat the Q-Ship down on a patch of ground that appeared free of lava.

Before the three disembarked from the ship, Eddie shot a look at Lars. "We'll wait for your confirmation. Be careful. And be quick."

"Yes, sir." Lars saluted before hurrying off in the direction of the security facility.

"Ready for some fun?" Eddie shot a look at Julianna.

She smiled easily, a spark in her eyes. "You know I am." She pressed the button on the box on her belt and disappeared.

"Damn, that's fucking cool." Eddie did the same, disappearing as well.

Aircraft Warehouse in Kezzin Battlebase 57, Planet Yit, Seolus System.

It was like walking inside an oven. Eddie kept his breathing steady. Heat exhaustion was a real issue he'd experienced during his stints on planets on the fringe. There was a reason shit was cheap out there. Most didn't like hanging out in hell.

Sweat puddled at his lower back, but he ignored it. The guard duty was light at this time of the morning. They couldn't complete this mission at night because they needed the hangar door open. That was key for pushing the crates out of the facility and to the rendezvous spot. However, they still had to be silent. Leaving tracks were another concern, but if they were fast then it shouldn't be a problem.

Eddie slid up next to the warehouse, Julianna adjacent to him. They waited until Lars relayed over the comms that he'd disabled the sensors.

"That was easy," whispered Eddie.

Lars responded over the comms. "Not if you were me. I keep getting strange looks, but there's so much personnel here, I don't think my unfamiliar face is that big a deal."

"Unfamiliar? You ugly aliens all look the same," said Eddie.

"Teach." Julianna's tone was punishing.

"I mean, Lars' has pretty eyes, more so than those other lizard people."

"I'll forgive your comment this time," said Lars, ignoring Eddie.

"Thanks. We'll get moving." Eddie peeked into the open warehouse. Engineers and soldiers bustled around, but most appeared distracted by coming or going.

"The meeting upstairs just started," a voice said.

"I'm heading that way. Just need to finish this up," someone else replied.

Eddie slipped into the warehouse, knowing he couldn't be seen. He made a beeline to the location of the crates. As reported, they were four by four and stacked on pylons. They'd have to push them out of the warehouse, but at least the path was clear, although far, to the Q-Ship.

Eddie pulled a handful of cloaking devices from the bag on his hip. He twisted one to activate the technology and stuck it to the side of the crate, where it adhered immediately. The crate of parts flickered but didn't disappear.

Julianna was nearby, trying to make her own crate of supplies disappear. He couldn't see her exactly, but the two devices stuck to the side of her crate gave it away, since she was invisible as well.

Eddie stuck another device onto the side of the large box. Again, it flickered but remained solid.

Third time's the charm, Eddie thought, quietly sticking another device on.

The crate of roughly five-hundred pounds suddenly disappeared.

Then, it reappeared, flickering briefly as it slowly rose a foot off the ground, and then it sputtered and faded completely, going invisible.

Bingo, Eddie thought. Julianna's crate levitated and disappeared a second later, too, matching his own.

One of the aliens called from across the warehouse. "I'll be up there in a moment. I just need to retrieve the schematics on that new ship."

Eddie almost slid behind one of the crates, but remembered he was cloaked. A moment later, a Kezzin wearing overalls covered in grease trudged past the supply area. He picked up a pad on a workstation and strode off, hesitating momentarily. He straightened, his back tensing, turned his head stiffly, and stared at where Eddie, Julianna, and the invisible crates stood. The alien's brow furrowed, some concern in his eyes. He took a step in their direction.

"Gin, are you coming?" called a voice from far away.

The alien tilted forward, narrowing his eyes like something was wrong. He turned his head in the direction of the voice. "Yeah, I'm coming." The engineer shook his head, then continued back toward his friend.

"We need to be fast," whispered Eddie.

"Copy," said Julianna.

Eddie leaned his weight against the crate, pushing it through the space. It lurched forward, easily gliding down the aisle and into the oppressive heat of the outside. Red cracks, flowing with lava, ran along the ground, sending heat toward his feet. Eddie moved swiftly, conscious to not make a sound.

Julianna signaled Pip right on time, opening the hatch for the Q-Ship. Eddie loaded his crate, sliding around just in time to give Julianna the space to push her crate up the ramp and into the ship.

"Two down…" he whispered to the empty space.

"Two to go," replied Julianna.

They bounded out of the ship and back to the warehouse just as the Q-Ship soundlessly took off, flying to meet the shuttle where crew members would unload the crates and send them to QBS *ArchAngel*. If they only got those crates to the main ship, then they were in great shape. However, anything else they stole would put a wrench in the Brotherhood's production. The more Q-Ships Eddie had, the better his squad would become.

Sweat ran down Eddie's head, dripping into his eyes. He ignored the hole in his boot from the damn lava. One more misstep and his foot would take the burn. He'd have to ask Hatch to make socks out of the new armor.

Despite the inconvenience, they successfully loaded four more crates onto the Q-Ship in only a few short minutes. *Not bad,* thought Eddie, once they had the equipment loaded.

Eddie slid behind his next target, a crate halfway toward the back of the long warehouse. He'd have to push this one farther than all the rest.

Footsteps echoed across the concrete floor, making him straighten. Engineers and mechanics had bustled by as they worked, but all of them were too far away for it to be an issue.

"The main meeting is letting out," said Lars in his ear. "I can only keep the sensors down for another couple of minutes. The staff member I'm covering for will be back from break in a moment."

Now or never, Eddie thought. He saw a cloaking device slap onto the side of the crate next to his. Julianna was already hard at work.

Eddie pulled his own device from the bag at his hip, placing it on the side of the crate. In quick succession, he slammed two more devices onto the box, but it didn't disappear like before.

"Those meetings are soul sucking," a voice rang nearby, drawing closer.

"Tell me about it," another voice sang.

Eddie froze behind his crate, sensing the pair were just in front of them. He couldn't push his crate out until they cleared the space.

"Gin, what are you looking at?" asked someone.

"The supply crates..." Gin said, stepping forward.

Eddie stuck his head out to find the Kezzin from before narrowing his eyes in Eddie's direction, although he couldn't see him.

"What about them?" asked the mechanic behind him.

"I could have sworn there were more," said Gin.

"Oh, man, the heat is getting to you," said the other Kezzin.

"I'm not kidding. Before I thought something was off, but now I'm certain of it." Gin's voice drew closer.

The other Kezzin laughed. "Crates don't just disappear. You're imagining things. They say it's the lava. It can play tricks on the mind."

Gin shook his head, pulling his gaze away. "Yeah, maybe you're right."

"Come on," said the Kezzin. "Let's grab something to eat before we've got to get to work."

"Sure," said Gin, absentmindedly turning, but keeping his focus on the crates.

"Fuck," whispered Eddie into the comms.

"Fuck is right," returned Lars. "You have one minute to get out of there before I've got to flip back on the sensors. I'll meet you at the Q-Ship."

"Copy," replied Eddie. He grabbed the last two devices in his bag and stuck both on the crate. It levitated and disappeared along with the one beside it. He pushed it forward, but then slammed into the crate. Something was wrong. Eddie threw his weight into the crate and it reluctantly moved. It felt off balance as it pushed forward.

The crate suddenly made a *shushing* sound as he pushed it. Eddie halted, looking down. The crate was leaving a scratched path that would only get worse, the further he pushed.

"You're dragging," said Lars in his ears.

"Damn it, that's too loud," he whispered.

"I've got you covered. Give me a second," Lars' voice rang over the comms.

A hand reached out and wrapped around Eddie's wrist, pulling him over a few feet. "Take my crate," Julianna said, barely audible.

That was a good idea. The crate would be heavier if it was dragging and Julianna would make quick work of it, ensuring it didn't rest on any lava long enough to get damaged.

A second later, a static filled the air in the warehouse. It was loud at first, accompanied by a screeching noise.

"Important informational updates," a voice began overhead.

"What's that?" asked Eddie, pushing the crate in front of him forward.

"The updates. They're prerecorded and play every morning. Looks like they already ran, but they'll just think it's a glitch that they're running again. Get going," said Lars over the comms. The speaker made just enough noise to cover the shushing sound made by Julianna pushing the crate.

"Nice," whispered Eddie, throwing his weight into the crate as it slid over the threshold of the warehouse. He turned, putting his back into the crate. A path snaked after the crate that Julianna had taken over. The scratching sound was drowned out by the voice relaying updates through the overhead speakers.

A head ducked out from a door on the side of the warehouse. "Why are the announcements playing—"

The figured stepped out of the room completely, his eyes on the path left behind by the crate. It was the same

Kezzin who had been suspicious before. He spun around, his fist clenching by his side.

"Sound the alarm!" he yelled through the open room.

The announcements seized. Lars must have been out of the security room or he'd been caught. Eddie sped up, his feet working double time to push the crate farther, faster.

An alarm sounded, ringing through the base. The crate Eddie was pushing flickered, and then became solid.

"Fuck," said Eddie. He turned to look over his shoulder. Armed soldiers spilled out of the warehouse and the surrounding buildings. Their eyes fixed on the crate sitting on the edge of the field bordering the aircraft facility.

"Get out of there! Your location has been compromised," said Julianna over the comms. She must already have loaded the ship with her crate.

The ship was only twenty yards off.

Soldiers charged in Eddie's direction, their guns at the ready. One line took aim at the crate but didn't fire. There wasn't anything but a stack of supplies to fire at. Then a figure broke free from the line of armed guards.

"Stop! In the name of the Brotherhood, I order you to stop!" a Kezzin yelled.

Eddie was about to abandon the crate and haul ass for the Q-Ship when he recognized the guard. It wasn't a crazy protective soldier trying to stand up for the Brotherhood. It was Lars!

Eddie slammed his weight into the crate, pushing it quickly over the next several yards. Then Lars joined him, and the crate sped forward, reaching the ramp in only a few seconds. Easily, they slid it up the ramp, and as soon as they'd cleared it, the ship lifted into the air. Shots rang out at that same moment as Kezzin fired in their direction.

The ramp closed as they finished pushing the crate into place. Breathless, Eddie stumbled for his seat. Julianna was already in position, controls for the guns in her hand.

"Oh, thanks for joining us, guys," she said.

"You didn't think I'd keep you waiting, did you?" he asked.

"You could have left that crate behind," said Julianna.

"Well, thanks to Lars, I didn't have to." Eddie strapped himself in. "And thanks for taking my crate that malfunctioned."

"You're welcome."

Eddie looked Julianna over. She wasn't even sweating, unlike him. "You made that look easy."

"Well, you handled the crates pretty well for a normal human."

"Mostly normal." Eddie took over the controls from Pip.

"We have a missile headed in our direction," informed Pip.

"They're sending a missile blindly out, hoping to hit us?" asked Eddie.

"No, from internal messages, I learned the Kezzin have heat seeking missiles," said Pip.

"Fuckers figured out another way to deal with our cloaks," said Eddie, igniting the thrusters and pivoting the ship to the side.

Julianna locked onto the missile and sent a rocket after it.

"Three more missiles have been deployed," said Pip.

"That's fine. If they want to play, we'll play." Julianna let loose a barrage of rockets, all locked on the missiles.

Eddie had been flying steadily, waiting for Lars to finish strapping the crates into place.

"All secure," sang Lars, popping into his seat and strapping on his safety belts.

"Party time is what you mean!" Eddie tapped the button, initiating the second thruster. He pulled back hard on the control, rocketing the ship upward at a sharp angle before rolling it to one side.

"Yeah!" rang Julianna, scanning the radar. "All clear on rockets, Pip?"

"All clear," affirmed the E.I. "That was fun!"

Eddie gave Julianna a sideways look, a question in his eyes as he leveled the ship out, setting the coordinates for QBS *ArchAngel*. "Yes, Jules, that was *fun*, wasn't it?"

The strange look Julianna gave Eddie mirrored his confusion. An E.I. didn't label experiences fun. He must just be copying the excitement of the crew.

"Pip, what else did you learn when scanning the internal messages?" asked Julianna.

"There were specs for a large weapon called a tri-rifle. It has the capabilities to kill, stun, and destroy. The range of the weapon supersedes our current weapons," informed Pip.

"Fuck! That sounds like a valuable weapon. It must be the one Ray De'ft is selling to Vas," said Eddie.

"That's why we'll have to be the ones who get our hands on it. Also, we could use a new weapon. I'm pretty tired of having to use outdated guns just so we're not tied to the Federation," said Julianna.

"Agreed, Whiskey."

"Did you just call me Whiskey?" asked Julianna.

"I'm trying out call signs."

"Keep trying," she said.

"Don't you worry. I'll find the perfect one for you," said Eddie with an exaggerated wink.

"I'm certain you won't," she responded, smirking.

Lars leaned forward. "While stationed in the security facility, I learned the new commander is a Kezzin by the name of Tremaine Lytes."

"Do you know anything about him?" asked Julianna.

"Yes, unfortunately, he makes the old commander, Orsa, look like a nice guy. Tremaine's units are the ones who search out and force Kezzin to serve the Brotherhood. It appears his recruitment efforts have paid off for him and gotten him a promotion." Lars' voice was full of bitterness.

"We all know the Brotherhood serves General Vas," said Eddie.

Julianna nodded. "Now we just have to find out who *he* works for."

"You think Vas works for someone? How do you know this isn't just a part of his evil plans?" asked Eddie.

"Everyone works for someone," said Julianna. "Even the Federation works for the colonies. The colonies work for the people. It's a reciprocal system. We just have to find out who is the most powerful in their cycle and take that one out."

"Damn, Jules, that makes sense. I like the way your brain works," said Eddie.

"Then you should remember that I hate being called Jules," she responded, cocking her brow.

Eddie winked. “We both know you like it. I can tell.”

“Oh?” she asked. “How’s that?”

“If you really didn’t like it, you’d deck me every time I said it,” he answered, grinning.

She couldn’t help but laugh. “Fair enough.”

10

Landing Bay, QBS *ArchAngel*, Paladin System.

The crew had already unloaded the crates the Q-Ship delivered to the shuttle. Hatch tapped on a pad, reviewing the supplies. He brought his eyes up to stare at Eddie and Julianna when they disembarked.

"How'd we do, Doc?" asked Eddie.

Crew members pulled the two other crates from the back of the Q-Ship.

Hatch eyed the new additions and pursed his mouth. "This will do, I guess."

"Aw, are you still mad about the booster? I brought back the ship in pristine condition this time," said Eddie.

"That's yet to be determined." Hatch bustled over, doing a rough inspection of the Q-Ship.

Jack strode across the landing bay, the crew members he passed straightening to attention. "As you were," he said. He halted in front of Julianna and Eddie, his eyes studying the crates. “Nice work. Six crates. That should do it. Were you spotted?”

“Not with any discernable information, but one of the crates did lose its cloak, which gave us away,” said Julianna.

“Probably placed the cloaking device wrong.” Hatch hurried over to the two crates that had been unloaded from the Q-Ship.

Julianna cleared her throat, straightening. “I placed those myself. You said the technology wasn’t one-hundred percent reliable.”

“That I did, Julie. My apologies,” said Hatch.

“Hey, why don’t I ever get any apologies?” asked Eddie, frowning.

“Because you’re an idiot.” Hatch busied himself, checking over the supplies.

“Commander Fregin, have you uploaded the information Pip acquired from the stronghold?” asked Jack.

Julianna was quiet for a moment before nodding. “He said that the transfers to *ArchAngel* will be completed within the hour.”

“Very good. I’m certain we’ll have access to a lot of important information,” said Jack.

“Yes, we already have some details on the weapon that’s trading hands, as well as having identified the new commander for the Brotherhood,” said Julianna.

“Well, I’d say that was a successful afternoon. You and your team deserve a break. We will be arriving at Onyx Station in a few hours. Why don’t you all take a day off to rest up? Enjoy yourself. As soon as the details on the meeting with Ray De’ft are confirmed, then you’ll be off again on another mission,” said Jack.

"Sir, have Chester and Marilla made progress with finding the meeting location?" asked Julianna.

"Not yet. But the meeting is in three days, and I'm confident we'll have enough information to intervene by then. In the meantime, you all wash up and take some R and R."

"I think the chief is implying we should get drunk to celebrate." Eddie leaned over and whispered loudly in Julianna's direction.

She gave him an irritated look, scrunching up her nose. "I think he's implying that you need a shower."

"Hey, lava makes me sweat. Sue me."

Julianna lifted her arm and sniffed. "Same goes for me. Blasted lava. What a horrific planet."

"Yeah, why can't the Kezzin pick a nice beach resort for one of their bases?" joked Eddie.

"That actually reminds me, there's supposed to be a new bar on Oynx, one that has a surfing simulator," said Julianna.

"What's surfing?" asked Eddie.

"Damn, you're sheltered," Julianna said with a laugh.

"I just need you to teach me, Jules. Teach Teach, would you?" he asked, clasping his hands together like he was begging.

"Tough luck, pal!" she said, waving a hand and taking off.

"Oh, come on! Teach Teach! That's funny shit!" Eddie cast a look back at Lars, who was helping to move the crates. "Let's go, Lars. We've got drinks to drink and bar fights to fight."

"Captain Teach..." Jack said with a warning on his face,

looking totally serious.

"You know I'm kidding, Chief!" said Eddie.

Wave House. Deck 26. Onyx Station, Paladin System.

The three strolled into the restaurant, which strangely had sand on the floor.

"Why would they put sand on the floor?" asked Lars, stepping carefully like he was walking on lava again.

"It's to round out the experience of being on a beach. It's called ambiance," said Julianna.

"Oh, that makes sense, although I've never been on a beach," admitted the Kezzin.

Eddie tapped Lars on the shoulder, leaning forward. "Be careful, she'll call you sheltered."

"If you only heard the things I called you behind your back," Julianna said with a half-smile.

"Damn, this woman is cold," said Eddie, frowning.

"Only to the people who matter the most," said Julianna, winking at him.

At the back of the restaurant was a large slide covered in water, with jets at the bottom that created a steady wave. A guy started forward wearing only trunks and carrying a flat oval shaped board. He stepped into the water at the arch of the slide, setting his board down. He stepped onto it and rode down towards the jets before catching a current and riding back towards the arch. From there, he cut the board to the right and left, riding the water in a way Eddie had never seen before.

"Damn, that's far out shit," remarked Eddie, his mouth hanging open.

"Just wait until you try it," teased Julianna.

"No way! I ain't doing that," he exclaimed.

"Not until you've had a few drinks, you're not," she said. "You can't surf sober. That's the rule."

Eddie ambled over to the bar, flanked by Julianna and Lars. He leaned on the counter, scanning the bottles against the wall. "Tonight calls for something special."

"You always say that," said Julianna.

"I haven't known you long enough for you to know what I always say," remarked Eddie.

"Oh, it just feels like a long time." She smirked.

"We'll take three Baba Yaga's Vengeance," said Eddie to the bartender.

The man lifted an eyebrow, looking surprised. "You want...three of those? Are you serious?"

Eddie thought for a second. "Yeah, you're right! Never mind. Let's make it six."

The bartender gawked for a moment. "A-Are you sure?"

"Let's go, barkeep," said Julianna. "We've got the night off and there's liquor to drink."

"Baba-what?" asked Lars.

"You're going to love it," said Eddie. "Burns like a mother!"

The bartender lined three glasses up and poured orange syrup into them. Then he filled the rest of it with a thin emerald green liquor.

"Yeah, I guess that doesn't look too bad," remarked Lars.

The bartender pulled a lighter from his pocket and lit the tops of the three drinks, shoving each forward as he did. "Next round coming up after you finish this one," he said.

Eddie picked up two of the drinks and offered them to Julianna and Lars, waiting until they took them. He grabbed his own. “Despite what you say, Julianna, there’s no one I’d rather be out in the field with.” He clinked his flaming glass against hers. “And Lars, you’ve proven yourself more times than I can count. Good work today!” He clinked glasses with him before all three brought their glasses together in the middle.

“Cheers,” they said in unison. They blew out the flame burning on the top.

Julianna hesitated, sniffing the liquor. “It doesn’t smell too bad.”

“It tastes a whole lot better than it smells.” Eddie threw his head back, taking the whole glass in one swallow. It tasted like burnt sugar.

Eddie slammed his glass on the bar. “Ready for round two.”

Julianna took a cautious sip of her Baba Yaga’s Vengeance before drinking down the rest. “Not bad. I guess sometimes you know what you’re doing, Teach.”

Eddie winked. “Damn straight. Now, are you any good at this surfing thing?” He pointed in the direction of the simulator where a new participant stood, reluctantly holding a board. The guy shook his head and charged forward, throwing down his board and jumping onto it. One leg shot up in the air and the guy teetered backwards. He recovered his balance, but his legs were locked out, his arms too straight on either side of him.

“This isn’t going to end well.” Eddie grabbed the second drink the bartender had made, blowing out the flame before it could burn off too much of the alcohol. That would be a shame.

"I fear you're right," said Lars, still sipping on his first drink.

"The key is to flow with the waves. Become one with the water. When the rider resists the water or hesitates, then they lose their balance," explained Julianna.

The surfer tanked, falling down hard on his tail bone, his board slipping out in front of him. It hit the jets, spraying the crowd with water. Shouts of complaints jeered from the onlookers as they shielded their faces from the spray.

Eddie handed the drink from the counter to Julianna. "Sounds like you know a lot about this surfing business. Why don't you show us how it works?"

She blew out the flame on the top of the drink. "I would, but I just washed my hair."

"If you don't wipe out, I think your head of pretty hair should be just fine."

"That's true. I just don't want to make you guys look bad," said Julianna.

"Such a sweetheart, this one." Eddie reached down and pulled off one of his boots before ambling forward and pulling off his sock. He kept walking as he took off the other boot and sock, leaving them in his path. "I'll show you how to do this."

Eddie, pulled off his shirt and threw it to the ground as he made his way to the simulator.

Julianna turned to Lars, a mischievous smile on her face. "Well, that was a hell of a lot easier than I thought it would have been."

"I kind of figured the captain would be game for such a challenge. He doesn't seem to scare easily."

"That he doesn't." Julianna motioned to the bartender who acknowledged her with a nod.

Eddie was leaned over, rolling up his jeans. He rose to a standing position and stared back at the pair by the bar. He beat his bare chest with one hand, making a sort of barking sound.

Julianna and Lars both laughed easily. "He still doesn't know what a dog sounds like, does he?"

"It would seem. We're going to have to get Harley to bark for him," said Julianna.

Eddie took the surfboard handed to him and climbed to the top of the tank, where the slide started.

"Are we taking bets on how long he'll last?" asked Julianna.

"I'm not sure if that's the respectful thing to do. He's my captain and—"

Julianna cut Lars off, slapping a bill on the bar. "I'm giving him seven seconds."

Lars smiled. "I'll take four."

Eddie stood ankle deep in the current-filled water, gauging it. Then he ran forward, throwing the board down as he jumped on to it. He and the board rode to the bottom where he had one glorious moment where he looked like he'd hold his own. The board shot straight into the jet, sending a surge of water over it, sinking it at once and sending Eddie to his tail bone.

Drenched in water and brandishing a wide smile, Eddie rose to his feet, the board tucked up next to his waist. He held his hand in the air and shook his head, sending droplets of water over the crowd. This time they cheered.

"Again! Again! Again!" they encouraged.

Julianna slapped down another bill. "Six seconds, this time."

Lars gave her a sideways look. "Four, still."

"Damn, should I inform the captain that you have so little faith in him?" asked Julianna.

"It's not a matter of faith. Things like surfing are rarely picked up easily. He's got to fall a few times to figure out how the board moves and how he should respond accordingly. I'd say after the fourth or fifth time, he'll have this down, and that will still be faster than most."

"That makes sense. So you're saying we all have to fall sometimes, is that right?" Julianna sipped her drink.

"Falling down is key, as well as getting back up. About like that." Lars pointed in Eddie's direction. He stood back in the starting position, nodding his head to the hum of the music and the chanting of the crowd.

"I don't disagree with that logic."

Eddie was slower this time to wade out into position. He dropped the board, stabilizing it with one foot as he watched how it moved with the current. Then he jumped onto the board and rode it down to the bottom where he wiped out after a few seconds.

Lars picked up the bills on the bar. "And if we're honest, I've got a lot more faith in that man than I've had in most throughout my life. Eddie has heart, which is not something that can be taught. It's inborn."

"Well put," said Julianna, finishing her drink.

Eddie had already taken the starting position again, not even needing to be encouraged by the crowd this time.

Julianna finished off a few more drinks, while Lars sipped on a single one as they watched Eddie try and fail. The fifth time Eddie took the position on the top of the simulator, Lars pointed, with his tumbler in his hand. "Now watch this time. My money is on him staying up for a good twenty seconds."

Finally feeling the buzz from the liquor, Julianna stared intently at the wave pool. The crowd was super charged, chanting and egging Eddie on. He stepped out into the water, a smile on his face, but his eyes focused. He stood to the side of the slide, not in the middle. After a moment he set the board down and jumped on it in one swift movement. He rode down and nearly lost his balance before righting himself. Eddie kneeled, placing his hand in the top of the water until the board backed up so it rode on the apex of the wave. From there, he stood taller, pivoting the board one way, and then the other, cutting through the water, handling the wave easily. It was like when he was flying. He seemed to understand how to harness the water and the air.

Julianna picked up her glass and held it out to Lars. "Well, cheers. You seem to be a master at reading these situations."

"Maybe. Or maybe I just got lucky." He clinked his glass against hers as Eddie continued to ride the wave.

11

Lower Deck Corridor, QBS *ArchAngel*, Paladin System.

"Is it normal to feel like my head is full of lead?" asked Lars, trudging through the corridor alongside Eddie.

"Actually, sounds like you didn't drink enough. I woke up feeling like a jackhammer was going off in my head." Eddie held out his palm, a small pill lying in it. "Take this and you'll thank me in five minutes."

Lars didn't hesitate before picking up the pill and swallowing it dry. "Thanks. I'm guessing Julianna didn't need a pill like this. She didn't even appear buzzed after all those drinks."

"You've guessed right. The commander will look so fucking chipper it will be ridiculous."

"Nano technology is something else," said Lars.

"It also gives me incredible hearing so I know when you're talking about me." Julianna rounded out of a connecting corridor, striding next to the pair.

"See." Eddie tossed his head in her direction. "So fucking chipper."

Lars studied Julianna. "It's a marvel, for sure. How do I get this nano transformation done to me?"

"You have to pretty much die, but be hanging on by a tiny thread," said Julianna.

Lars laughed. "Yeah, never mind. That seems a little extreme."

"It is. The line between life and death is miniscule, and most cross over to the other side before they can be helped."

"Well, and also only someone like General Reynolds could authorize such a transformation," said Eddie.

"Or the Empress, as in my case," said Julianna.

Lars eyes widened with awe, Eddie noticed.

"Lars, the commander and I are going to track down this weapon. I'm leaving you behind on this mission." The three paused outside of the Intelligence Center.

Lars nodded. "I'll focus on flight training."

"Yes, do that, but I have something else I need you to do," said Eddie.

"Yes, sir. What is it?"

"You know I've been sorting through files for recruits, picking personnel for the crew," said Eddie.

"I'm aware of that," affirmed Lars.

"I'd like you to review some files and make some choices on crew members."

"Sir? You want me to recruit for the QBS *ArchAngel*? Isn't that a big job?" asked Lars, surprised.

Eddie nodded. "Yes, it is. It's just until we get this

weapon. I don't want the recruitment effort to slack. Jack is adamant about us filling up this ship."

"But that's an important responsibility, recruiting personnel."

"And I trust you will do a good job with it. You have an instinct for people. Use that," said Eddie.

Lars looked to Julianna, who was standing tall, hands pinned behind her back. Then he returned his gaze to the captain. "Absolutely. I'll devote my full attention to the job."

"I trust you will." Eddie turned, striding into the Intelligence Center.

Chester tapped his foot to the music playing, something with a strange electronic beat. He looked deep in thought as Julianna and Eddie entered the Intelligence Center.

"The chief said you had information for us on the meeting with Ray De'ft and Doka," said Eddie. He leaned down and petted the animal with knots of shaggy brown hair.

The dog always seemed to be everywhere on the ship. Wherever Julianna was, that mutt could be found, almost like it was stalking her. Most people's face lit up when they saw Harley. His presence had been a welcome one on the ship. However, not for Julianna. The memory wasn't clear, but it still tightened her chest. Canines. Growling. Julianna running as fast as her child legs could take her. But now, she was super human. Why should the old memory still affect her?

"Thanks to Marilla, I was able to decode the communications I picked up off the Trids' defense network. Pretty tricky system they use," said Chester, spinning around in his swivel chair, facing them.

"It's not a logical code, that's why most can't figure it out. However, my years on Kai are paying off," said Marilla. She wore an easy smile and looked quite at home sitting behind one of the six desks behind Chester's main work-station.

"All of the Trid correspondence looked like chicken scratch to me." Chester wheeled around and typed a few keys on his keyboard. He punched the enter key with his pointer and leaned back. "I replaced a few of the characters based on Marilla's input and voila!"

The data on the largest screen above rearranged until it said something that was recognizable.

"Dillon?" asked Eddie. "That's way the hell out there. Like the fringe of the fringe."

"I believe that's in the Lorialis system where we found you, Teach." Julianna said it like she was unsure, but she wasn't. Her brain didn't make it so she'd forget such things. It catalogued all data with accuracy.

"Way the hell out there, like I said," admitted Eddie.

"I couldn't make sense of the meeting location, but that's where Marilla further helped," informed Chester.

All heads turned to the communications officer. She stood, striding over to a screen of a large map of Dillon. "The location of the meeting with Doka and Ray De'ft is planned for the East Bawah Tanah system over here."

"I've never heard of that," said Julianna, the location not ringing any bells at all.

"Right. It didn't make sense to me either. We couldn't

find anything remotely close to that in this area. However, I dug deeper and learned something interesting. This part of Dillon is a huge industrial area that has a complex network of underground tunnels. Then this sparked a thought. In their native language, the Trids don't have a word for underground because they...well, they have no reason to be underground. Their natural habitat is the water. Land is a recent part of their evolution. Bawah Tanah as far as I've been able to tell is a new translation for subterranean."

"So the meeting is in the east area of these underground tunnels?" asked Eddie.

Marilla nodded.

"Damn. We're going to storm in on a secret meeting to steal a giant gun inside a tunnel, with limited places to go. Doesn't sound difficult," said Eddie, pretending to be intimidated, but Julianna caught the excitement under the surface. This was a damn hard challenge, and he loved the idea of it.

"Be sure to wear your armor, Teach," said Julianna, striding out of the Intelligence Center with the damn dog following her.

Loading Dock 03, QBS *ArchAngel*, Paladin System.

Hatch drummed one of his tentacles against his lip, thinking. He tilted his head to the side, like looking at the Q-Ship from a different angle would answer his question.

"Pip?"

No response, as usual. Hatch stared around the loading bay, as if he were looking for the E.I.

"Pip, are you there?" There was a hint of worry in Hatch's voice.

The screen on the wall flickered to life and *ArchAngel* appeared, blinking back at Hatch. "I'm here. How may I assist you, Doctor A'Din Hatcherik?"

"I didn't ask for your assistance," said Hatch grumpily. "Where's Pip?"

"Do you prefer Pip over me?" she asked.

"No." Hatch answered too quickly. "That's ridiculous. Preference plays no part in it. He's an E.I. and I only needed his input."

"I'm sure I can be of help to you. What is your question?" *ArchAngel* asked.

"Doctor A'Din Hatcherik, you requested me," said Pip suddenly.

"There you are. Where were you?" Hatch paced back and forth, an anxious feeling in his gut.

"I was with Julianna. I apologize for the delay."

Of course, Pip was with Julie. She was his first priority, since he was in her head. It was something Hatch envied about the commander. She was never alone and always had assistance.

"Am I no longer needed?" asked *ArchAngel*.

Hatch huffed. "You were never needed, you nosy body. Go on, then."

"I do not believe either of those descriptions fit me very well. I am neither nosy, nor do I have a body. I am concerned by your avoidance. Should I call someone to watch over you, to make sure you don't hurt yourself?" asked *ArchAngel*, and then the screen went blank before Hatch could answer.

"How may I help you, Doctor Hatcherik?" asked Pip, his voice light and welcoming.

Hatch waddled up to the Q-Ship. The front end was open and wires exposed. "Do you have the schematics for the first Q-Ship I built?"

"Yes, of course I do. I have access to all of those records, but so does *ArchAngel*."

"That's neither here nor there." Hatch dismissed this with a wave of his tentacle. "Compare those plans to the ones the Federation used when they created this Q-Ship."

"Do you spot an inconsistency? Is that why?" asked Pip.

"I don't, but that's the problem. I know there has to be a discrepancy. The gate technology isn't quite right in this version. My instinct tells me they followed a different protocol when constructing the gate engine for this Q-Ship."

"I'm running a full comparison of the two different schematics. All differences will be logged and sent to your pad," said Pip.

"Thank you." Hatch picked up the electronic pad sitting nearby, pulling it to him with his long tentacle.

"Can you tell me something?" asked Pip.

"I can tell you a thousand things? Can you be more specific?"

"Of course," said, Pip, a bit of humor in his voice. "How does instinct work for you?"

Hatch brought his eyes up, away from the pad. "Oh, well, that's a good question." It was an intuitive question, one of many that Pip had been asking lately. "Instinct is when you know something without knowing it."

"Like a gut feeling?" asked Pip.

"Yes, exactly. Sometimes we operate automatically with instinct, like how a baby Londril knows how to move, walk and swim from the beginning. It's built into our DNA."

Pip was silent for a moment. "There are species of turtle that once hatched, know to head straight for the ocean, away from predators. Is that a good example of instinct?"

Hatch nodded. "Yes, all species have something they do to survive that is a part of instinct."

"However, when you mentioned instinct, it was more of a feeling. How do you know to trust a feeling?" asked Pip.

Hatch thought for a moment. As a scientist, it did seem strange to trust feelings, and yet many of Hatch's most valuable technological achievements had been because he was led by instinct. An inkling, a little feeling.

"Our feelings are incredible biofeedback devices that can direct us if we allow them. However, one must not allow feelings to overwhelm them. Only listen and respond accordingly," said Hatch, staring back down at the pad.

"Bingo! I knew it. The Federation followed my schematics for building the Q-Ship, but then used their own when constructing parts like the gate drive." Hatch bustled over to the Q-Ship, finally feeling as though he'd made progress after being stalled for a long time.

"Why is that a problem?" asked Pip.

"Because my process for the gate was created specifically for the Q-Ship. The QBS *ArchAngel* has its own gate technology, but it doesn't suit something like the Q-Ship. Good thing the captain hasn't had a chance to jump in this Q-Ship. He might have ended up toast," said Hatch, digging into the wires in the front of the Q-Ship, making sparks fly.

"That is a good thing," said Pip.

The loading dock grew silent, punctuated only by the sounds of wires sparking and bolts falling to the ground.

"Doctor A'Din Hatcherik?" asked Pip after a long minute had passed.

Hatch pulled his head out of the front compartment. "Yes?"

"Will you tell me more about feelings?" asked Pip.

Flight Training Center, QBS *ArchAngel*, Paladin System.

New recruits halted and saluted Commander Fregin as she passed them. She nodded, stalking to the back of the long room lined with flight simulators. It wasn't until she retrieved the pad with the flight training stats that she realized she was being followed.

Turning, she gave the mutt a sinister glare. Harley tilted his head to the side with a soft, talkative bark.

"No dogs in the training room." She shooed him away with a wave of her hand. He fled for the other side of the room, staring back at her.

You don't like him, said Pip in her head.

Is it that obvious? Dogs belong in parks and with old ladies who live alone. Not on a ship. When did this place turn into a fucking zoo?

I didn't find anything about dogs in the rules and regulations for the QBS *ArchAngel*.

Don't you sass me on this.

Does that mean you're allowing for me to sass you on other things going forward?

I'm about to show you sass.

What is it about the dog that you don't like?

Besides the fact that it sheds, takes up resources, and serves no purpose?

Yes, besides all that.

Julianna swiped through several of the reports, scanning the averages. The new recruits were performing well. They'd be ready once the new Q-Ships were built, whenever that was.

You didn't answer the question completely, observed Pip.

Didn't I? I'm fairly busy and preoccupied.

You've already reviewed those reports twice today.

Julianna let out an audible sigh. *They change hourly.*

From my observation, the dog increases the mood and morale of those on the ship. I also have research that suggests pets increase serotonin levels in the brain.

What do annoying E.I.s do? Decrease serotonin?

Ouch. Now you've taken off the gloves.

Did you just say ouch?

I think I did. That statement was meant to hurt, am I right?

I guess so. Did it hurt?

I'm still processing. I believe you meant it in jest, but I could still observe where it could hurt based on the impression that you didn't like me.

Pip? Julianna leaned against a workstation, her legs stretched out in front of her.

Yes, Julianna?

You're saying the strangest things lately.

Am I? I hadn't noticed.

Julianna studied Lars' report. He, of all the new fliers, was doing the best. Teach would be happy to hear this.

Do you need anything else from me?

No, why?

Doctor A'Din Hatcherik has requested my assistance.

Go on then. Julianna set the pad to the side to find the dog standing next to her legs, looking up at her.

"I thought I told you to get out of here."

Harley whimpered softly in reply. He lifted his chin in the air and eyed her.

"What do you want?"

The dog laid his head softly on Julianna's legs. She narrowed her eyes at the gesture but didn't shove him off.

"I don't see what everyone likes about you."

Harley rubbed his head back and forth against Julianna's leg, begging for attention.

"Does that shit work on everyone else? You're such an attention whore."

He pulled his head off her leg and lifted his foot and pawed at her.

She almost smiled. This one was persistent. "You know we have work to do here? I can't have the crew getting distracted because you need your head scratched. I already have to keep an eye on Teach. Don't you make more work for me."

Harley backed up, his eyes sparkling. He barked playfully.

"Oh, you're so fucking ridiculous." Julianna stretched to a standing position and stalked for the exit, Harley trotting after her, tail wagging.

12

Q-Ship, en route to Dillon Planet, Lorialis System

The Q-Ship maneuvered around an asteroid belt, slipping easily between two giant meteors.

"Ever notice that the crappy systems always have more asteroids?" asked Eddie, pulling back on the controls.

"Pip, what's your insights on that? What do your records show?" asked Julianna.

"What classifies as a crappy system?" inquired Pip.

"Stale beer and the ugliest aliens," said Eddie.

"I've taken an analysis of all the systems in my database and ranked them based on economy and educational standards—"

"There he goes with his computer-talk again," interrupted Eddie, talking in a whisper.

"Those highest on the list do not in fact have less asteroid belts than those ranking lower," informed Pip.

"Man, you kind of take the fun out of things sometimes. I was just saying—"

"However," continued Pip, cutting Eddie off, "the systems I've superficially judged as crappy based on Julianna's experiences definitely have more asteroid belts."

Julianna and Eddie exchanged curious looks. "Did he just say crappy?"

"He's been saying all sorts of strange things lately, ever since Hatch upgraded him." Julianna pointed at a planet ahead of them. "There's Dillon."

"I have not been saying strange things," argued Pip.

"Pipe down, Pip. We've got a big gun to steal from a fish," said Eddie.

"Pip, lock the Q-Ship on the coordinates for the Bawah Tanah system. We need to park the Q-Ship close to one of the main entrances into this underground network." Julianna eyed the screen, waiting for the navigational route to update with Pip's coordinates.

"What's taking so long, Pip?" asked Julianna after a moment.

"You forgot to say the magic word," said Pip.

"Now?" asked Julianna.

The screen remained unchanged as the Q-Ship slipped into Dillon's atmosphere.

"I don't think that's the word he's looking for." Eddie laughed.

Julianna's eyes darted away, looking distant for a brief moment, and then she smiled, staring down at the screen. "There we go," she said when the navigation updated.

"Did you just threaten Pip?" Eddie asked, flying the ship further to the surface of the planet, which was dry and barren.

"Maybe," chirped Julianna.

"Man, this is one ugly planet," said Eddie. "Seriously, the next meeting with the Trid we interrupt needs to be at a five-star resort. Some place with paper umbrellas in the drinks."

Julianna lifted one eyebrow, staring at Eddie. "For some reason, I have a hard time picturing you with an umbrella in your drink."

Eddie scoffed. "I'm in touch with my frilly side."

"No, you're not," she said, laughing.

"Yeah, you're right. I'm not. But at least I can surf!" Eddie set the cloaked Q-Ship down on a stretch of sandy land next to a manhole that led straight to the Bawah Tanah system. "Tell me, Jules, where would you like to vacation when we get our next break?"

She seemed to think for a moment. "The Libra system has a planet that's covered in geothermal pools of water. They're supposed to be incredibly refreshing and restorative."

"You're enhanced with nanotechnology. Why do you care about swimming in healing water?" asked Eddie.

"I don't, but they're a really cool blue color and the planet is cold, but the waters are warm. I hate being hot when I'm sitting on a beach," said Julianna.

"Yeah, I could get behind that. Personally, I want to sit in the woods for a few days. There's something about trees and nature that's relaxing."

"That will have to wait. Instead, we're trekking through underground tunnels." Julianna jumped out of the ship.

Eddie did the same, activating his cloaking belt at once and disappearing from view. "Alright, you remember the plan?"

"Sneak up on a Trid and steal his gun, right?" she asked.

"Yep, keep it simple." Eddie lifted the metal lid, peering down into the dark tunnel. The smell of dirty water hit his nose. "At least it's not a sewer, like before. Hopefully that trek through the Kezzin sewers with Lars was the first and last time."

Julianna lowered herself into the tunnel using the ladder, then she activated her cloaking belt and disappeared. "Try having an enhanced sense of smell."

"No thanks." Eddie followed behind her, ensuring that the area outside of the tunnel was still clear.

Their way ahead was mostly dark, lit by lamps every fifteen feet that hung from the ceiling. Julianna and Eddie set off slowly, their boots making noise as they trudged through the shallow water on the ground.

"Hard to sneak up on a gang of Trid when we make so much racket," said Eddie.

"Ray De'ft is expecting Doka. He will just think he's approaching. We'll have him cornered before he knows what hit him."

"I hope it's me who gets to hit him."

"You don't even know the guy. Why would you want to punch him?"

Eddie shrugged. "A guy who sells a dangerous weapon in a dark tunnel just seems like he needs to be punched."

"Yeah, you're probably right," admitted Julianna.

The pair fell silent as they neared a split in the tunnels. Several metal doors lined the walls.

"Pip has access to the electronic communications in the area," said Julianna.

"Picking up anything juicy?" asked Eddie in a whisper.

Julianna didn't answer for a long moment. "Apparently, Trids are sort of boring."

"Boring? Is that what the E.I. said?"

"Yes, he says it's mostly boring communications. However, he thinks he's located Ray De'ft. He should be up here in roughly fifty yards. Follow my footsteps."

"Copy," said Eddie, watching the splash of water in front of him. At the split, the displaced water on the tunnel ground led to the right. Without warning, the splashing stopped. Eddie halted.

"Trid up ahead. Stationed outside the second door. You want him or shall I?" whispered Julianna.

"Ladies first," replied Eddie.

"Stay here."

Eddie didn't answer but, instead, squinted in the darkened tunnel. His eyes had adjusted now. Julianna probably saw clearly and could make out the guard stationed up ahead. She'd be faster approaching, too, not alerting him.

There was no splashing of water. Just a *thud,* and then Julianna said. "All clear."

Eddie sped forward. On the ground, in front of a door, was a large Trid slumped over.

"How'd you run without creating any splashing?" asked Eddie, staring around, but not seeing Julianna.

"I ran on the side of the tunnel wall."

"Oh, of course you did," said Eddie sarcastically.

"And I knocked out this guy before he even knew I was there. He'll have an awful headache later, but he's still alive."

"Okay, well, the next one is mine." Eddie kicked the gun

next to the passed out Trid away, making it slide farther down the tunnel.

Julianna must have grabbed the wheel on the door and cracked it to the left. It turned, and then the seal on the door broke and it pulled back.

"Bobby, you got Doka there?" a voice called from the other side. "That guy is late."

Eddie, still cloaked, slipped through the opening of the door, Julianna after him. On the other side was a round room, a bit brighter than the tunnels due to a grate where sunlight filtered through. A Trid, wearing a suit and an angry expression, stood at the back of the small room. Beside him was a large case.

Eddie caught the guards standing on either side of the door way before they ran into him. The first guard was about to duck through the door to find out who had opened it. Eddie shot his fist forward, straight between the Trid's eyes. The alien fell back toward the wall, but recovered quickly. Julianna, by the sound of it, was handling the other guard.

"What the hell is going on?" asked Ray confused by the sight of his guards getting the shit beat out of them by nothing he could see.

Eddie swept the legs out from under the Trid, throwing his elbow straight into his gut. He yelled as the wind was knocked out of him. The guards head fell back hard into the metal floor, knocking him out.

Ray was unfastening the case. Eddie spun around just as he pulled out a giant gun, which looked heavy as hell and fucking menacing.

"Show yourself or I'll shoot and ask questions later.

This thing has a wide span and won't miss," said Ray, his tone hot with anger.

Eddie flipped the switch on his belt and held up his hands as he materialized. "I believe you're a man of your word. I'm not here to kill you. I just need that gun you're holding."

"Where's Doka?" asked Ray, his eyes scanning the area around Eddie. Julianna was still cloaked.

"Doka met an unfortunate end. He asked me to retrieve the gun for him," said Eddie.

Ray's black eyes tightened. "I was ordered to not sell this gun to anyone but Doka."

"Plans changed. Oh, and I can't buy the gun. I'm just going to be taking it." Eddie said, his hands still raised. He noticed the water on the ground displaced slightly as Julianna edged forward.

Ray laughed loudly. "You stupid human, you think I'm going to give you this? You have some nerve."

"You have no idea."

Ray tilted his head to the side. "We have intruders. Back up immediately," he said into his comm device.

"Oh fuck. Why did you have to do that? I thought we could have been friends," joked Eddie. Why hadn't Julianna knocked this guy out yet?

"Who else is with you?" asked Ray.

Eddie shrugged, daring to lower his hands. "Just me. Where'd you get that gun?

Ray eyed Eddie, motioning backward with the gun. "Take a few steps back."

"But then I can't see the gun."

"If you don't step back, then I'm going to show you

exactly how it works." There was a small splash of water beside Ray. His eyes dropped to the right. "What's going—"

The Trid keeled over, the gun flying up and to the side as he did. His face fell flat to the ground, partially obscured by the standing water. At least there wasn't any fear of him drowning, being a Trid and all.

Julianna materialized, holding the giant gun.

"Damn, it's about time. That guy was about to waste me." Eddie pointed to the large weapon in her hands.

"Oh, don't be such a baby. I had plenty of time to knock him out."

"I think you wanted me to get shot," teased Eddie.

"Right, because I want to drag your ass out of here along with this heavy-ass thing." Julianna pushed the gun in Eddie's hands. "We've got company."

"And I've got a giant gun, so bring it on." Eddie studied the gun quickly, trying to understand how it worked.

"Do not, I repeat, do not fire that thing down here. We don't know the first thing about the gun, and its ammunition could fire off these walls and blow us to Timbuktu." Julianna pulled back the door, peering around into the tunnel.

"Where is Timbuktu, by the way?"

"Far-the-fuck away. I think it's in the Axiom system." Julianna waved him out into the tunnel, pulling one of the blue marble-like grenades from the pouch tied to her belt.

"Is the coast clear?" asked Eddie.

"No, I'm just waving you out into an ambush," said Julianna sarcastically.

Eddie smirked. "Look who gets catty in battle."

Julianna looked around like surveying the room for another person. "Who?"

"Ha-ha."

The pair stepped out into the tunnel. "Backup is arriving from both directions according to Pip."

"Sounds like a party."

"Should we throw up our cloaks?" asked Julianna just as three Trid turned the corner in front of them, running in their direction.

"Or kick ass the old-fashioned way."

"Fine." Julianna pulled her gun from her hip, aimed it in the darkened tunnel, and fired off three shots. They all met their targets, taking them down at once.

"At some point, you're holding the big-fucking gun so I can play, too," said Eddie.

Another gang of Trids materialized behind them. "Time to go." Julianna turned the blue grenade and threw it in the approaching Trids' direction. Then she and Eddie took off, retracing their path back to the exit. A moment later, a loud popping noise filled the tunnel when the grenade went off.

Eddie and Julianna turned a corner in unison, nearly running straight into two large Trids. One grabbed Julianna by the shoulders, pushing her hard into the tunnel wall. Eddie brought the large gun up like a bat and slung it across the face of the other Trid, slamming his head to the side. He swayed, and then fell over, crumpling against the wall.

"Don't...use...unknown...gun...as...weapon." Julianna said each word in between ducking the Trid's attacks.

Eddie looked the gun over. "You worry too much. I can't shoot the thing and now I can't swing it around."

Julianna bounced on her toes, ducking under one of the Trid's arms and grabbing him around the neck from behind. "Accidentally set that thing off and I'm going to be pissed," she said, pressing hard down on the Trid's throat as he flailed. Finally, he slipped to the tunnel floor where he passed out.

"I think you broke a sweat there."

"Don't be absurd." Julianna and Eddie set off again, making it to the exit without meeting anymore Trid.

"Here, you take this and I'll go check for baddies." Eddie handed the tri-rifle to Julianna and climbed the ladder to the surface.

The Trid must have all been inside the underground because the path to the Q-Ship was clear.

"Let's get that gun back so we can find out what it does. I want a chance to shoot that thing," he said, exiting the tunnel.

13

Officers Lounge, QBS *ArchAngel*, Lorialis System

Eddie set his feet on a chair and leaned back, puffing on a cigar. He peered at his cards, then tossed a chip from his stack onto the center of the table.

Chester eyed Eddie closely. He was excellent at reading people, which made him an excellent poker player. "You know you don't have anything. That's why you're nickel and diming me."

Eddie chuckled. "If you know so much then put your money where your mouth is or fold. You know the rules, boy."

Covering his grin, Chester scanned the table. Lars had folded immediately. He didn't know that poker wasn't about playing the cards. He kept saying he had shit hands.

Eddie told him that the cards did not matter, but he didn't understand.

Julianna looked more interested in watching the group than playing, like she was cataloging everyone's different ticks and tells. This woman was an observer, and Chester guessed that made her a deadly warrior. Marilla had refused to play and lay across the sofa in the corner reading a book on her tablet, Harley curled up at her feet.

Chester picked up three of his black chips, twisting them in his fingers. He noticed that Eddie's eyes widened minutely, but he covered it by puffing on his cigar, blowing smoke up to the ceiling. He didn't want the bet to be raised, that much was obvious to Chester.

"Is anyone else falling asleep waiting for Chester to make up his mind?" asked Eddie.

Chester eyed his cards. It was a shit hand. He tossed the black chips into the pot.

A serious expression fell on Eddie's face. He seemed to think on this for a moment. Then he released a wide smile and threw his cards in the center. "Damn it, you got me again. Take your winnings."

Letting out a long breath, Chester rejoiced, pulling the chips to him.

"That makes five hands in a row he's won," observed Lars, sipping on a Coke.

It had been too long since Chester had a real Coke. This was one of the many benefits to being back working for the Federation. On the planet of Kemp, all they had was some shit called Dr. Pepper. Whoever that doctor was who invented that drink, they needed to have his or her license revoked.

"He's a damn card shark. But not like one of those Trids. A cool shark," said Eddie with a laugh.

Marilla lowered her tablet, a pursed look on her face. "I urge you to have more tolerance for the Trid species. Just because your target happens to belong to that species shouldn't reflect poorly on all of them."

Eddie turned, putting his forearm on the back of the chair. "Don't worry. I've met some pretty revolting humans, too. I get it."

"Trids are pretty ugly, though. We can all agree on that," said Lars, shuffling the deck of cards.

All faces turned and looked straight at the Kezzin with strange expressions.

"What?" asked Lars. "Oh, I get it. You ugly humans think I look strange."

"Strange doesn't sufficiently cover it. You have scales on your skin," said Eddie lightly.

"And you have a hairy face." Lars dealt out the cards.

Eddie rubbed his jaw. "Only when I don't shave. And Julianna doesn't have a hairy face." He paused. Looked at Julianna. "You don't, do you? Maybe you shave, too."

Julianna glanced at her cards and threw in a chip. "Teach, I say we arm wrestle after you lose all your chips."

Coupled with her beautiful facial features and strong persona, Commander Fregin was quite interesting to watch. Chester thought it was fascinating how this enhanced soldier tensed when Harley trotted by. There was a story there.

Eddie picked up a chip and tossed it into the pot. "Yes, to the arm wrestling contest. You'll beat me, but I wager I hold my own for a good twenty seconds."

Lars pushed his cards away, folding. "I'm out, but I want in on that bet. I wager it will be more like ten."

"Fifteen," said Chester, looking at his cards. It was actually a good hand. Full house.

"If the captain has another beer, then I'm betting less than ten," said Marilla from the couch.

Eddie turned around, a mock look of offense on his face. "I expect this kind of abuse from the others, but not from you, Marilla. I thought you had a heart."

She shrugged, pulling her tablet back up to read. "Being on the QBS *ArchAngel* is rubbing off on me. Soon, I'll be heartless."

"That may be for the best," deflected Eddie. He brought his mug of beer up, holding it toward the center of the table. "To being heartless."

Chester lifted his Coke and clinked it against the other's drinks. It was a funny toast because no one had more heart than Captain Teach. Although Chester had first met Eddie at gunpoint, Chester knew the man could be trusted. There was something in his eyes that spoke of his honor. Meet enough criminals and the good guys begin to stand out.

Chester threw in a stack of black chips. Julianna folded right away, leaning back in her chair.

"I'm all in," said Eddie, pushing all his chips into the pot.

Casting a sideways smile at Julianna, Chester said, "Get ready to arm wrestle. The captain is about to lose."

Loading Dock 04, QBS *ArchAngel*, Lorialis System

One of Hatch's tentacles stretched across the dock, clambering through a set of tools.

"Damn it. Where's the wrench?" he said from several yards away.

"It's behind you," said Pip.

All of Hatch's tentacles were busy holding something,

screwing in a bolt into the new Q-Ship or soldering wires in the main frame.

The Londil huffed. "Of course, it is." His free tentacle retraced and felt around behind him until it located the wrench.

"Why do you order all of the crew off of the loading dock when you're working like this?" asked Pip.

Hatch rubbed the back of his tentacle against his head before going to work with the wrench. "Because they'll distract me."

"Are you sure that's the real reason?" asked Pip.

Hatch looked up, surprised. "What kind of question is that?"

"I've observed that you only work like this when you're alone, using all of your tentacles to maximize efficiency. You never do such things when in the company of others."

Hatch gulped and busied himself by burying his head into the main compartment of the Q-Ship's engines. It was true that no one saw him work like this. No one needed to know that his secret to success was multitasking. Most of the crew only had two arms and two legs, but he had eight, which expanded the number of things he could do. If any of them saw him like this, they'd probably think he was even more alien.

Not that he minded, of course, but it was always better to lessen the divide between people. If he had to use two tentacles at a time while in the in presence of others, so be it, but the rest of his time would be spent using his full potential.

"I'm nearly ready for you to upload the interface software," said Hatch, his tentacles working separately like individual workers.

"When do you think this Q-Ship will be ready?" asked Pip.

"If I work without interruption, then in the next couple of days. However, that's probably too much to ask for, given how often the crew comes to me with problems."

"And once you have this one complete, you'll be ready to turn the updated schematics over to the crew?" asked Pip.

"Yes, I guess so. You're tracking the blueprint updates, right? I'm confident I can give them plans so they can build three more Q-Ships, at least."

"Doctor, speaking of distractions," said Pip. "The captain and the commander are headed to the loading dock. They will arrive in approximately thirty seconds."

Eddie rubbed his shoulder, grimacing with pain. "Damn, I'm gonna have to ice this."

Julianna smirked proudly. "You're the one who agreed to the arm-wrestling match."

Hitting the button for the loading dock, Eddie strolled forward when the door slid back into the wall. "Well, it was worth it. I now know what your call sign is."

"What's that?" asked Julianna. She'd slammed his arm down after a short five seconds. Who would have thought that the sweet communications officer was going to win the bet?

"Strong Arm. It fits you perfectly."

Julianna pursed her lips and nodded. "Yeah, that's not completely horrid."

When they approached, Hatch was fiddling with a small metal box with wires sticking out of it. Distracted, he looked over his shoulder, and then did a double take at them. "There you are. It's about time."

"You told us you needed a few hours to review the tri-rifle," said Eddie.

"I lied. I only needed an hour. The design on the weapon is fairly straightforward and easy to understand. It's powered by an internal sonic force." Hatch turned and waddled over to a set of targets he'd set up.

"Sounds so easy," said Eddie sarcastically.

"It's impressively constructed. I'll leave it at that." Hatch picked up the tri-rifle from the table. It was quite large in comparison to his size.

He turned and faced the targets in the distance. "The rifle has the simple technology to shoot single bullets." Hatch pulled the trigger and fired the weapon, not hitting any of the targets.

"Guessing you should stick to mechanics, Doc," said Eddie.

"This gun was designed to be shot by a Trid, not a Londil. I think it will be fine for you, Eddie, since you've got fish eggs for a brain."

"Fair enough," chirped Eddie.

"Like the weapons the Kezzin use, this one also has stun technology." Hatch turned a knob and pulled the trigger. A blue ray shot from the gun, also not hitting anything.

"I'm guessing if that would have connected with a target, then it would have stunned it," said Eddie.

"Do you want to walk out in front of me here? I'll test the stun option on you." Hatch waved Eddie over, a scowl on his face.

Eddie held his hands up in surrender. "I'm good, Doc. Sorry, please continue."

"I like the stun options. I was actually going to discuss having you create some stun rifles for us in the future. After being in the underground and having to limit the use of bullets, I think it could be helpful going forward," said Julianna.

"That's a good idea, Julie. I agree, and I'd be open to that project. Let me just finish the second Q-Ship first," said Hatch.

"Of course. Thank you," replied Julianna.

"That's a good idea. Thank you," mocked Eddie. "Why are you two nice to each other but treat me like I'm an imbecile?"

Julianna and Hatch both gave Eddie loaded expressions. "Ha-ha. Fine, I'm a space monkey. Show us more of the gun."

Hatch turned the notch again. "The most useful part of the gun is that it has the option to obliterate something with the density of a one foot thick concrete wall using a spray technology." Hatch moved several yards over until he was standing in front of a solid concrete wall, roughly five feet long. He aimed the weapon and shot. The wall split in half, the top crumbling and falling to the ground.

"Whoa. So it has a horizontal destroy option?" asked Eddie.

"Exactly, which I was able to tweak to create another option for the first two functions. Now the tri-rifle could be considered a quad-rifle, although I don't think that has the same ring to it." Hatch moved a switch on the side of the gun. Then he moved back over to the target area. "This new tweak can be used with either the bullet or stun options." He aimed and pulled the trigger. A ray of bullets shot from the weapon, taking down all of the targets. Hatch lowered the gun and turned, a proud smile on his face. "See, even a poor shot can be successful with this gun."

"Damn, that's far out," said Eddie, his mouth hanging wide open.

"And incredibly dangerous in the wrong hands," said Julianna.

Hatch shuffled over and handed the gun to Julianna. "Yes, but you're in possession of the tri-rifle so we can breathe a sigh of relief. Now we just have to keep it away from the bad guys."

14

Intelligence Center, QBS *ArchAngel*, Lorialis System.

Whistling, Eddie strolled into the Intelligence Center. Chester was leaning back in his chair, throwing a ball up in the air and catching it just before it smacked him in the face. Marilla seemed engrossed in her work, typing fast on her computer, leaning forward, close to the screen. She paused when Eddie entered the area, smiling politely at him.

"I've heard rumor that you've hacked into Doka's communications," said Eddie.

Chester caught the ball and beamed. He had a wide smile that seemed to take over his face at times. "You've heard correctly."

"Good work. Have you confirmed the meeting with Vas?" asked Eddie.

Chester fired a finger gun at Marilla. "That's where Pony Tail comes in."

Marilla pulled her focus off her screen, looking to

recover from deep thought. "I'm working on that right now. It has to be in the Trid's native language, so I'm checking to ensure I have my translation correct."

"I hear the Trid's language is complicated as hell," said Eddie.

Chester laughed. "It sounds like a series of gurgles. Forget about reading or writing it."

"It's intricate, with many different dialects that affect the meaning. Little nuances in the language make writing it a complex task. That's why I want to get the confirmation from Doka correct. He was from the northeastern hemisphere of Kai, which has a subtle difference in how verbs are used. Someone like General Vas, who is from the lower hemisphere, will pick up on any inconsistencies," explained Marilla.

"This hemisphere business is different," said Eddie.

"It's pretty interesting. Their cities are all underwater so that affects how they use locations. Mar was telling me all about it. Super strange," said Chester, throwing the ball back in the air overhead.

"What can you tell me about the colonies under the water? Their technology and ship construction? Do you know much?" asked Eddie.

Marilla shook her head. "Unfortunately, I was never granted access to their underwater lands. I heard rumor that they had some incredibly advanced technology. There's supposedly a giant facility just under the eastern equator. It's where their ships are all constructed."

"Ha! I've seen the Stingrays. Flying fish. They can't have any advantages over the Q-Ship," said Eddie.

Shrugging, Marilla focused back on her computer

screen. "I think this confirmation is good. I'll send it over to you, Chester."

"Chester, is that your real name or a hacker nickname?" asked Eddie curiously.

Chester shot forward, checking the screen just in front of him. "Keeping an eye out." He looked up at Eddie. "My hacker name is Monte Niles. Unfortunately, Chester is the name my parents gave me."

"I like your name," said Marilla. She blushed when Eddie and Chester looked at her. "I mean, it's different, but kind of a fun name. Fits your personality."

"Why thanks, Mar." Chester's eyes swiveled up to Eddie. "Apparently, I'm named for a city on Earth where my ancestors were from. My mother was also obsessed with *Alice and Wonderland* and said she named me after her favorite character."

Eddie smiled. He always liked to know these little tidbits about his crew. It made them feel more like family. "Haven't had a chance to check out those books. Maybe one day I will, and then I'll find this character you're named after."

"They may not be your style. Disappearing rabbits and angry queens," said Chester. "Okay, I've got your communications, Mar." He swiveled the mouse around on the screen before typing a series of passwords. Then he tapped one key and looked up victorious. "All done!"

"Oh boy. Imagine Vas's face when he's expecting to meet Doka to buy a big gun and Ghost Squadron shows up," said Eddie.

"No thanks. I'll fight from the keyboard and leave you guys to fight with the guns," replied Chester.

"Are you going to hurt him?" asked Marilla innocently. She was such a humanitarian. Well, alientarian or whatever it was.

"Only if he tries to hurt us, so yeah. Well, and it's because of him that we've lost the original Q-Ship. I've got to knock him in the head for Hatch. It's only fair," said Eddie.

Chester peered at the largest screen in front of his desk. "Looks like Vas is anxious for the meeting. He's already responded. I'm sending it over to you, Marilla. The rough translation looks promising, though."

Marilla scanned her computer screen. "Got it. Yeah, this looks straightforward. He confirmed the time and meeting place."

"Great. *ArchAngel?*" called Eddie.

A screen on the wall flickered to life and *ArchAngel*'s face appeared. "Take the coordinates from Officer Sours. Set the ship on course. We will prepare to jump at twenty-one hundred hours."

"Yes, sir. Anything else?" asked the A.I.

"I'll have more specifics once we strategize," said Eddie, waving to Marilla and Chester. "Good work, you two."

Flight Training Center, QBS *ArchAngel*, Lorialis System.

Lars climbed into the flight simulator. He had spent most of the day training and only took a break when Julianna kicked him out of the Flight Training Center and told him to go eat something. She was gone now, so he'd decided to sneak back and put in a few more hours. Men who are motivated by love will push themselves in ways that others won't. Lars gripped the controls, his thoughts on his family back on Kezza.

There were a few missions Lars had aced from the beginning. However, there was a particular space combat mission that he couldn't pass. Getting blown out of the sky always made Lars' heart palpitate, and this was only a simulation. The idea of extra planetary combat alongside a military force of similar and larger spaceships was chilling.

"I can do this," he said to himself, taking a steadying breath. "*ArchAngel*, load simulation Strike Zero."

"Loading Strike Zero," the A.I.'s voice called.

Lars slammed back in his seat as he accelerated the ship through the docking ramp. The Black Eagle shot out into the black space that sparkled with stars and distant moons. The flight simulator was top notch and made the experience of flying feel incredibly real.

He flipped switches on the deck as the ship came to cruising speed. "Carnivore on patrol. All looks good out here."

"Copy, Carnivore," said *ArchAngel*.

The simulation was always different, meaning that Lars didn't know when the strike would happen or how.

"Carnivore, three Stingrays just appeared on the radar. Enemy ships on your port side," informed *ArchAngel*.

"Coming to pick on the new guy, are they?" Lars swerved the ship in the direction of the Stingrays. "Where'd they come from?"

"That's unknown. They might have jumped," said *ArchAngel*.

"Stingrays can't jump." This was the thing about this stimulation that kept tricking Lars up. There were unexpected twists, ones he didn't anticipate. Julianna said that's why it was the most important one to pass. Nothing in space was predictable.

"It appears these Stingrays can jump," countered *ArchAngel*.

"You're just making shit up now. Trying to throw me every curve ball you can, aren't you?"

"It is my responsibility to present new challenges to you. Would you like another simulation?" asked *ArchAngel*.

"No, just Stingrays jumping seems a bit farfetched."

"My data shows there are many unknowns regarding this type of Trid ship. All I have is a model of the outside."

Lars activated the thrusters, adjusting his direction toward the three craft on radar. He slipped his finger over the trigger on the controls. The three Stingrays were now in his sights.

"Is there a reason you're not firing?" asked *ArchAngel*.

"How do I know they're enemies?" asked Lars.

"Because I informed you that they were." There was a hint of annoyance in the A.I.'s voice.

"Last time I checked, you didn't think for me. What if these are friendly Trids who are just passing through? Maybe they don't want any trouble. War is not inevitable among species. Sometimes it's an option."

"My records indicate that most interaction among Trid ships results in warfare," reported *ArchAngel*.

"Maybe that's because we shot first and asked questions second." Lars swerved the Black Eagle to the side of the Stingrays. It appeared that they were going to pass without provocation. Maybe they weren't the enemy in this scenario. From the side, he could make out the gray ship.

The nose was black, gills on the side and wings that represented fins. In the back, around the booster, were spikes. *Such bizarre looking ships,* he thought.

The three Stingrays had nearly passed when they suddenly turned, heading straight for Lars. All three fired.

"Damn it!" Lars rolled the ship to the left, taking a dive, quickly changing position.

"You were informed they were enemy ships," said *ArchAngel,* gloating.

"Oh be quiet!" Lars sped the ship to the other side of the three Stingrays before they changed position. The alien ships weren't as nimble as the Black Eagle. There had to be another reason behind their design then, but he didn't know what.

He pulled the trigger, firing a round of rockets. Two of the ships took damage, falling out of formation. The third pulled around in time to launch a missile at Lars. He spun the ship to the side, thinking he'd flee until he could position himself again.

"May I talk now?" asked *ArchAngel.*

"What?" Lars bit on the word, zooming in multiple directions, trying to put space between him and the Stingrays. Damn, those things were fast.

"You're holding your breath. Your heartrate is also elevated and blood pressure is rising," informed *ArchAngel.*

"I'm being chased by an ugly fish!" he yelled.

"However, in combat, you must keep your vitals even."

"Noted." Lars pulled back hard on the controls, bringing the Black Eagle up at a sudden angle. He flew upside down over the Stingray, yanking the controls down again until he had made a complete circle and was behind the enemy ship. He fired off several rounds, a few of them connecting with the Stingray, sending it spiraling to the nearest planet.

"Mission complete. Good work, Carnivore. Bring it home," said *ArchAngel,* sounding proud.

Lars let out a giant breath. "About damn time!" He threw a fist in the air, feeling victorious.

Bridge, QBS *ArchAngel,* Lorialis System.

Three more crew members had been added to the bridge, Eddie observed, scanning the area. It wasn't enough, but it was growing. They started with roughly forty and were now double that. Lars had made some good decisions when they'd left him in charge of the recruitment efforts. Now, Eddie was back on the job. This was what he and Julianna needed an XO for.

"Do you have good news for us?" asked Chief Renfro.

"The messages have been sent and the meeting with Vas is confirmed," reported Eddie to both Jack and Julianna.

Jack nodded, directing their attention to where the strategic table was located in front of them. "*ArchAngel,* bring up a rendering of the meeting location." A satellite image of the Harbor District spread over the table.

"Ah, damn fuck heads." Eddie's eyes widened. The satellite clearly showed that the Brotherhood had infiltrated the warehouse area where the meeting was located.

"Your meeting is here." Jack moved a blue chip over and placed it on a building in the middle.

"And they have it surrounded," observed Julianna.

"Exactly, so getting in there is going to be a real fucking

issue. However, taking out Vas isn't an in and out job. It appears they've set up a temporary base of operations in the area," said Jack.

"They're like a fucking fungus, taking over and spreading."

Jack nodded at Eddie, his eyes low. "I agree. We really need a squad to properly take this area."

"Yeah, we don't have one," said Eddie.

"No, but we can use what we have." Jack pointed to the area bordering the harbor. "There's a fleet of Stingrays stationed here. We need these guys in the air and drawn away from the warehouses. That way you aren't ambushed when you capture Vas."

"Capture?" asked Eddie.

Jack lowered his chin and regarded him with a hooded expression. "Yes, capture. Not as easy as taking him out. However, my intel informs me that Vas is working for someone else."

"Wait," interrupted Julianna. "We thought the Brotherhood was working for Vas and he was the powerhouse behind this."

"That's what we thought. However, I had Chester follow some account transactions for the Trid and it appears there's someone else funding this whole operation," stated Jack.

Eddie combed his fingertips over his chin. "So, we need Vas to talk."

"Orsa didn't talk when we captured him. He's still silent in the brig," said Julianna.

"Which makes me think you are losing your interrogation skills," joked Eddie.

Julianna shrugged. "Short of killing the Kezzin, I can't intimidate him any further."

"He's protecting someone. We have to hope that Vas will open up. Orsa has the Brotherhood to protect. I suspect the Brotherhood have something major to gain if they keep the head honcho's identity secret, but the deal is off if revealed," said Jack.

Julianna stared down at the satellite image. "Which is why Doka killed himself to keep the secret."

Nodding, Jack said, "The Trid must have a similar deal, hence all the account transactions."

"So how do we get Vas to talk?" asked Eddie.

"We make him a better deal than what he's got," replied Jack.

Eddie shook his head. "Didn't work on Orsa."

"And it may not work on Vas, but there's only one way to find out. Each man is different and has their own thresholds." Jack pointed to the center warehouse. "You two will meet Vas here. The new commander of the Brotherhood, Tremaine Lytes, has the area surrounded. Although taking out Lytes and Vas at the same time would be ideal, you're understaffed for such a mission. Instead, you need a separate diversion to draw the Brotherhood away, ideally to the north."

"So get the Stingrays to head to the south and the ground soldiers to the north. We're dividing up their forces," said Eddie, nodding. It was a good strategy as long as nothing went wrong.

"Yeah, and park hella close or if you get surrounded you're screwed." Jack picked up a small model of a Q-Ship. "Think you can land here?" He set it down in an alleyway at the back of the meeting place.

"Setting it down there would be extra tight, take precision, and incredible navigation. So, hell yeah. We can make that happen," said Eddie, winking at Julianna who pretended to ignore him.

"Very good. Be ready to set off just after we gate in." Jack turned and strode from the bridge.

Loading Dock 03, QBS *ArchAngel*, Lorialis System.

"She's a beauty, isn't she?" asked Eddie, arriving beside Lars. The Kezzin was admiring the Black Eagle parked just in front of them. As a single-flier ship, it was one-fourth the size of the Q-Ship. Eddie felt a fondness for this bird because it was where he'd spent a lot of his younger flying days. With the Q-Ship, he had the speed and agility of the Black Eagle, with many more bells and whistles.

Setting a Black Eagle down in an alleyway would be way easier than the Q-Ship, like he'd have to do before ambushing Vas. But they couldn't take Vas with a Black Eagle. They needed a drop ship for that. And the Q-Ship could be cloaked, which was key.

"Yeah, it's a bit surreal to stand in front of this ship. It's hard to think this is what I'm flying during the simulation," said Lars, his eyes pinned on the ship.

"I heard you aced your final simulation," said Eddie, proudly.

Lars shrugged, looking a little downtrodden. "Actually, I didn't ace it. I got docked for not immediately treating the foreign aircraft as enemy ships."

"Oh, excuse me. You took a moment to use your own judgement. Never mind. You more than aced it. You get extra credit for that."

"*ArchAngel* wouldn't agree with you. She's the one who grades."

Eddie scoffed. "*ArchAngel* doesn't know what she's talking about."

"I *can* hear you," *ArchAngel*'s voice chimed.

"Well aware," chirped Eddie. "My point is, Lars that ArchAngel is knowledgeable, but she went into the mission with prejudices."

"My programing makes it impossible for me to be prejudiced," argued *ArchAngel*.

Eddie ignored her. He was actually endeared to the A.I. She had spunk. "Lars, I admire your optimism. We should be open to the idea that foreign ships won't always be aggressive, but vigilant enough that we can respond if they react with an attack. That's what you did."

Lars brought his eyes up, a small smile in them. "Thank you. I'm going to run the simulation a few more times and see how I do. Maybe I can improve my score."

Eddie clapped Lars' on the shoulder. "That sounds good. But you can only learn so much from a simulation. I can't pass you until you actually fly."

Lars rotated his head around, his eyes widening. "Wait. You… You want… Me-me-me…"

"Yes, I think you need to take this Black Eagle out. Once you've had a successful run, then I can pass you and authorize you to join us on our mission."

"You mean the one going after Vas?" asked Lars, disbelief in his expression.

"That's the one! We need someone to distract the Stingrays, pulling them away from the mainland."

"You think I can do that?" asked Lars.

"I do, but you've got to prove it by taking this bird out for a spin. Are you ready?"

Lars face broke into a wide smile. "Absolutely!"

15

Captain Teach's Private Quarters, QBS *ArchAngel,* en route to Axiom System.

Sinking down on to the couch, Eddie let out a long sigh. He needed to sleep...well, nap. Cat nap, he guessed. Eddie didn't know why the term was called that. Maybe one day he'd meet a cat and know. That's what the QBS *ArchAngel* needed next! A cat. Julianna would be fucking pissed then. The ship would turn into a zoo, and she'd be raving mad. She was kind of cute when mad. Well, always really, but she got this little indent between her eyes when mad that Eddie sort of liked. Maybe that's why he tried to get under her skin.

Eddie ordered a special bottle of whiskey to celebrate Lars completing flight training. However, since they were a few hours away from the mission, his first mission, the bottle was going to have to wait. This one was a special bottle of whiskey. He lifted it closer and read the back label.

QBS's brew master spent over two years working with new alien strains of barley and maize from planets in the system's inner ring—barley from the uninhabited Ballistia and maize from the capital planet Chainex. Officers of the Federation were tired of other teams having all the fun creating new drinks and sources of revenue and, therefore, challenged the brew master to create the Federation's first new hard liquor. Development had been mildly problematic but nothing a couple of weeks in a pod doc couldn't fix. The Ballistia strain was too sweet to be useful for anything but a candy-ass hard liquor and the Chainex strain puckered you up tighter than a duck's ass. Together, they were perfect, a classic combination of sweet and sour that engaged both palates of the tongue. Only downside: they were both deadly. Hence, the two subsequent years of R and D.

The brew master had never actually become a tester, claiming he felt his work was too important. In reality, he was simply afraid of dying from the effects of the alcohol. While they could science the fuck out of the strains and make them safer for consumption, it seriously fucked with the taste. Mother Nature just wasn't having it. Eventually, another tester had poured a shot into the brew master's empty Pepsi bottle as part of a practical joke.

Before he had any time to react or even pray that the station's A.I. would notify someone and get him to the pod doc in time, the dopamine dumped, the rush of pure grain alcohol, and the whole reason for all the R and D, overwhelmed his system. Even as his nanites raced to counter the reaction, the brew master was on top of the world, flat out drunk, and horny as hell. Unfortunately, he was all alone and couldn't figure out how to get out of the chair, much less the distillery. It was a long twenty-five minutes until his nanites had countered all the effects and he realized that he wasn't dead, much to his own amazement.

When the brew master's report was complete, and the A.I. continued its testing, it was found that the trace remains of Pepsi had neutralized both strains, allowing for proper consumption of the new beverage.

It was then that the most potent whiskey in the galaxy was created. The Federation presents **Dead Man Walking**, a Queens Bitch's Space Whiskey.

Eddie laughed to himself. Catch Vas and find out who the bad guy was behind all this. Then he could crack this baby open and drink until he was a dead man walking. Might sound scary to some, but Eddie liked the adventure. The universe was a fascinating place. Everything had the potential for thrills, even whiskey.

He placed the bottle back on the side table.

"*ArchAngel,* wake me up in an hour, would you?"

"Are you sure you want to rely on me?" asked *ArchAngel.* "I don't know what I'm talking about, remember? What if I wake you up at the wrong time? What is an hour, anyway? Maybe I don't know."

"Oh, did you get your feelings hurt when I was talking to Lars? I was just trying to make him feel better. And you shouldn't have downgraded him for making that call." Eddie yawned, resting his hands over his abdomen.

"What if it had been you telling him to fire on enemy ships and he refused, wanting to see if they were truly deadly?" asked *ArchAngel.*

"I would have skinned his ass if the ships didn't blow

him to bits." Eddie settled back deeper into the couch, his eyes closing.

"Exactly. Ignoring a superior officer to follow instinct is never okay. I simply held Lars to the standards that are set forth."

"True, but I might have been okay with checking out the enemy ships first. Why don't we just agree to disagree," said Eddie, his words slurring from the sleep taking over his brain.

The room fell silent until Eddie's snoring filled the air.

"And yes, maybe my feelings did get hurt," said *ArchAngel* in almost a whisper.

Loading Dock 04, QBS *ArchAngel*, en route to Axiom System.

Checking over her gear, Julianna turned and headed straight into the loading dock. In the distance, she spied Hatch bustling around the Q-Ship, his tentacles going in eight different directions. He didn't know she was approaching due to her soft steps, and he'd completely change his behavior once he realized she was there.

Don't you tell him I'm here, she said to Pip in her head.

As agreed, I will prove myself dishonorable and not alert Doctor A'Din Hatcherik to your presence.

I believe you're only obligated to be truly loyal to me.

And I am. However, Doctor A'Din Hatcherik knows how to downgrade my software or disable me altogether.

Speaking of that upgrade you recently received, when do you want to talk about the changes?

What changes? asked Pip, trying to sound innocent.

Oh, are we playing a game? Alright, let's pretend that you're not different.

Different how? I don't know what you mean?

Pip...

Yes, Commander? How may I assist you?

Julianna smiled to herself. *I'd like you to talk about your feelings. Can you do that?*

I'm sure I can. I don't know what you mean about feelings. I have data that I can report, observations I can make, and correlational data I can provide. Other than that, I do not offer subjective information like these feelings you're referring to.

Uh-huh. There was a knowing tone to Julianna's voice, but she didn't say anymore. This evolution wasn't going to happen overnight, nor did it need to be acknowledged completely yet.

Julianna was standing only a few feet behind Hatch, whose tentacles were each performing different tasks. She cleared her throat. He straightened. All of his tentacles retracted until only one was screwing a bolt into place.

After a few seconds, Julianna cleared her throat again. Hatch turned his head over his shoulder, catching her. "Oh, you're there. I didn't notice."

So many keeping secrets, Pip. What's up with that?

I don't know what you mean. What secrets is Doctor A'Din Hatcherik keeping?

That's cute. Let's keep up the charades a bit longer. It's fun.

You're speaking nonsense, Commander.

Am I?

I'm going to run systems checks on the Q-Ship's mainframe.

Yes, good idea.

Julianna brought her eyes to Hatch, amusement playing in her gaze. "Is the ship ready to go?"

"I believe so." One of Hatch's tentacles picked up a rag and absentmindedly polished the side of the ship behind his back.

"I would tell you not to worry but—"

"Things that happen in a battle are never predictable. It shouldn't be your place to reassure me that my Q-Ship will return unscathed. I've been thinking about it…"

"Yes?" Julianna prodded.

"I was attached to the first Q-Ship, the one that was blown up."

"As you should have been. That was a ship that took you years to construct. The finest of its kind."

"But a ship nonetheless. It can be reconstructed, that I'm certain of now," said Hatch.

"Well, I'm relieved to hear you say that since we will need many more going forward. However, I think your disappointment over the loss shouldn't be diminished. This is your work, and what we're doing for the Federation, well, it's our legacy. Some go on to have children who carry on for generations. Some fight and create and innovate so that the future generations can survive. Don't you ever think that what you create shouldn't be grieved when it's destroyed? That would be undervaluing your genius, and none of us aboard the *ArchAngel* would dare to do that," Julianna finished with a supreme tone of finality.

Hatch made to nod, but then his eyes skirted to

someone over her shoulder. “Anyway, as I was saying,” he said overly loud, obviously trying to control a rogue emotion. “Chief Renfro asked that I innovate a strategy that will draw the Brotherhood away from their positions and to the area to the north.”

“Why are you yelling?” asked Eddie, sidling up next to Julianna. He placed his arm on her shoulder and leaned, placing entirely too much of his body weight on her. She stepped to the side, making him stumble a bit before finding his footing.

Hatch’s cheeks puffed out. “I was simply stating that I’ve got a new set of bombs for you all to place. Remember the bombs that I gave you the last time, when you were supposed to bomb the weaponry on EXA, but got caught?”

“By Lars, if you remember,” said Eddie with a laugh. It was funny that the Kezzin soldier who caught and imprisoned Eddie and Julianna was now their best newbie pilot. Julianna had agreed with Eddie’s decision to pass Lars right away when she saw his simulation results. It had been her idea to include him on the mission, which she hoped was a good one. It was scary offering officers opportunities to prove themselves, knowing they could get themselves killed. That was the price of fighting for a secret detachment of the Federation. It all came with great benefits and huge risks.

“As I was saying, I think that if you use the same bombs, it will distract the Brotherhood. You’ll have to land in the district to the north, set the bombs, and then remotely trigger them once in the air. It’s the best diversion I could come up with,” said Hatch, starting to pace.

“I think it’s a good plan. Most of the Brotherhood

soldiers will be sent to the bombing site, which will take them away from the area around Vas." Julianna smiled approvingly at Hatch. He knew he was a genius, but she thought he didn't want anyone to know how incredible he was because then he'd lose an edge, the ability to surprise.

Hatch nodded, the prior emotion before Eddie walked up absent from his face now. "Very good. The bombs are already stocked and ready for placement on the ship."

"Thanks, Hatch. You're the best," said Eddie, exuberantly.

Hatch puffed up his cheeks and turned, putting his back to them. "Just bring…" he trailed away, scuttling off several yards. Then he said, "Just don't screw up."

16

Q-Ship, Axiom 03, Axiom System.

Wearing the armor Hatch had made for them, Eddie and Julianna were prepared for battle. The tri-rifle sat in a case behind the cockpit. They were planning on bringing it to the meeting as Vas was expecting it. However, the Trid wasn't getting his hands on it, but he would see how well it worked firsthand.

"What's your twenty, Carnivore?" asked Eddie over the comms.

"Black Beard, I've just entered the atmosphere," said Lars.

"Relax. You got this," encouraged Eddie. The tension was heavy in the Kezzin's voice.

"Yeah…"

"How's the Black Eagle handling?" asked Julianna.

"Like a dream," answered Lars.

"That was Strong Arm's way of checking on you. Don't

take it personal that she's not more encouraging," said Eddie.

Julianna cast a scowl at Eddie, looking about like she was done with his shit. She wasn't though, he knew.

"You're a natural, Carnivore. Get in there and do what we planned," said Eddie.

"Copy," said Lars, and then the line fell silent.

Eddie flipped a switch, muting the line. "He'll be fine," he said, mostly to himself.

"We passed him. He's prepared for this," said Julianna.

"We both know that nothing prepares you for battle and space combat."

"Except for combat itself. Simulations can only do so much."

"Yeah, let's hope it was enough."

"Whatever happens, Teach, you have to know we prepared him the best we could. It was his decision to go on this mission. We'll carry our men on our backs if we have to but, eventually, they stretch their wings and have to fly on their own," said Julianna, sounding more sympathetic than he'd ever heard her.

He looked at her and nodded, there was a meaningful expression in her eyes.

Harbor District. Trinidad City, Axiom 03, Axiom System.

Armed soldiers marched through the alleyways between the buildings in the Harbor District. Julianna observed from the air that the Kezzin seemed to be preparing for something. It was in the way they moved, like getting ready for a deployment. She was familiar with the way an army moved and knew the signs well.

Eddie set the cloaked Q-Ship down in an empty field. In the distance, the warehouses in the Harbor District could be seen, flanking the gray waters.

"Blowing up an empty field seems kind of boring," said Eddie, staring out at the brown grass waving in the air.

"I'm sure it will only get more interesting as time rolls on." Julianna unfastened herself from her seat, grabbing the bombs.

"I'm in position," said Lars over the comms.

Eddie flipped a switch. "Very good, Carnivore. We are too. Wait for my signal."

"Copy."

Julianna opened the door and marched out into the open field. A bullet whizzed by her face. She ducked back into the cloaked ship. "Damn it! We have enemy fire. Pip, do you have satellite yet?"

"Affirmative. Checking now for cause of attack," said Pip.

"Now that's more like it. Much more fun than blowing up an empty field," said Eddie.

Julianna pulled her pistol from her holster. "Glad you got your way. Hope you're happy."

"It appears motion detector guns have been set up around the perimeter. The Q-Ship took a few bullets upon landing," said Pip.

"These guys are getting more and more prepared for our tricks," said Julianna.

Eddie picked up the tri-rifle. "Not all of them."

Julianna smirked. "Let me go first. Cover me."

Eddie nodded, both of his hands on the tri-rifle. He aimed it out the side door, around the Q-Ship.

"Closest guns set up at your two o'clock," informed Pip.

Eddie closed one eye, scanning the seemingly empty field. Julianna cast him one last look before diving and rolling through the tall grass. Several shots tried to follow her. She heard Eddie fire three times. Julianna, propped up on her elbows, spying smoke wafting in the air.

One target down, Pip said in her head.

How many more are there?

At least three. The problem is they only raise up when they catch movement, keeping them nicely hidden. There's one due west.

So we can't take them out unless one of us baits them?

I'm afraid so.

Looks like it's my day to be the minnow. Julianna caught Eddie's attention, waving to the motion-detector gun at her back.

He nodded, aiming his new toy in that direction.

The spray technology might be good for this.

And it could be haphazard. I've never been a fan of spraying off shots with the hope of hitting a target. Not to mention that a barrage of gunfire is one way to draw attention to our position too early.

I concluded that you were right when I ran the scenario, which is why I didn't suggest it first. However, you as bait is less than ideal.

Ah, shucks Pip. I didn't know you cared.

Of course I do.

Pip was an E.I. He shouldn't care. And Julianna shouldn't care that he did or didn't. The whole thing kept bringing up uncomfortable memories. She shoved them away.

Julianna took in a steadying breath and popped up. Several gunshots fired off. She side-stepped moving fast before rolling back into the grass. Her head popped up, looking at Eddie. He held up two fingers, then pointed down.

Two down. One to go.

Last one is at your nine o'clock. It's farther than all the rest. Going to take a precise shot to take it out.

Julianna silently indicated that direction at Eddie who nodded in confirmation, aiming the gun.

Crawling sideways, Julianna slithered through the grass until she was on the other side of the ship. The last thing she needed was to pop up and have Eddie catch one of the bullets aimed at her.

Open the hatch on the other side of the ship.

Done. You're going to run around the ship?

It's the only way to give Teach a sufficient chance to knock it out based on the distance.

Good plan.

Okay, well, on the count of three. One.

Julianna crouched on her knees.

Two.

She pressed her fingers and toes into the ground, ready to spring up.

Three.

Julianna jumped to a standing position, zipping to the side and sprinting. Bullets ripped through the grass around her, spraying through the air. She cut in around the Q-Ship, not safe from the bullets until on the other side. She flung herself into the open ship, the door closing behind her at once.

Eddie lowered his weapon, looking relieved. "I got the last one."

"Good," said Julianna, breathless. Her arm stung suddenly. She peered down, surprised to find not just one, but two bullets embedded in her armor. Pulling them from the lightweight material, Julianna smiled. She held up one of the bullets. "Damn, Hatch is a fucking genius."

"Yeah, we owe him big," said Eddie, beaming. "Ready to place some bombs?"

"Yeah, imagine what Commander Lytes will think when he discovers the field is bombed and his fancy guns have been shot down."

"I'm hoping he's pissed as hell." Eddie gauged the field again before stepping out, holding the tri-rifle. "I've got your back."

"I've got the bombs." Julianna reached into the bag on her hip, pulling one of the small bombs from it. She set each of them roughly ten feet apart. When all of them had been placed, she returned to the ship.

"That was fast," said Eddie, sounding impressed.

"Yeah, well, the fun hasn't begun yet. Let's get in the air." Julianna jumped into her seat, fastening herself into it.

"Some fancy footwork back there."

"I suppose so. I used to be a ballerina."

"Really?" Eddie's face was full of surprise.

Julianna rolled her eyes and laughed. "No, not really." Maybe she'd dreamed of dancing on a stage at one point over the last two-hundred years, but life had served up something different for her. Something better. Something that made sense to her. In her next life, if there was one, she'd do something creative, if just trying to survive wasn't the chief mission.

The Q-Ship rose off the ground, the boosters taking it up fast. Julianna stared off to the bay where rows of Stingrays could be seen in the far distance. There were more than there'd been when they studied the satellite image. She flipped the comms switch.

"Carnivore, are you ready?"

Static filled the radio before it cleared. "Ready," called Lars over the comms.

"Your turn. We'll detonate once you're done," she said.

"Copy."

From a row of clouds, Julianna watched as a Black Eagle dove toward the fleet of Stingrays. With her enhanced vision, she noticed many of the Trid on the ground look up at the sudden disturbance. She suspected that pilots would be radioed, orders given.

"Only a matter of time until the sky is full of those fish ships," said Eddie, staring at the same sight, although his view wouldn't tell him as much.

"Let's hope Lars can lure them off. The last thing we need is a fleet of those fuckers interrupting our meeting."

"He will." Eddie sounded confident. And why shouldn't he? Lars had passed flight training with top marks. The problem was he was their only flier. This mission really needed more like six Black Eagles, and Eddie and Julianna both knew that but had been reluctant to admit it.

She offered him a cautious look just as several Trid ran out, sliding helmets on their heads as they boarded their ships.

"Looks like it's show time," said Julianna.

Lars' first flight had been incredible. Cruising by stars and moons was a trip. His chest had tightened with an emotion he'd never felt. Pride wasn't the right word for it. They had a word for it in the Kezzin language. It meant "feeling like a god." Flying had given that to him. However, flying along the surface of this planet was different. Less freeing and more intimidating.

Dipping the nose of the Black Eagle, Lars' dived straight at the field of parked Stingrays. He pulled up at the last minute, leveling out.

"Come on you ugly ships. Let's play," said Lars.

Behind him a volley of shots flew through the air. He swerved, pulling one wing of the ship up just in time to miss the hit. Three Stingrays were already on his tail after only diving a few times at the ships. "Oh good. You decided to come out and play. Let's go."

Lars jerked the controls to the side, taking the Black Eagle over the gray waters of the harbor. He punched it once over the open waters of the Fumi Sound. Mountains stretched across the coastline in the distance, a place for Lars to give these ships the slip. By the time they knew what was happening, Eddie and Julianna would be in position.

"They've taken the bait," said Lars over the comms. He checked the radar. "I have six Stingrays on my tail."

"Sheesh, Carnivore. Punch it. You're in the wide open right now," said Eddie over the comms.

A spray of fire shot around Lars' ship. He dipped down, moving the ship the way he'd done on the simulations. It was better in real life. The controls of this Black Eagle responded better, like he and the ship were one. He never felt born for anything in particular...until now.

"Get to the mountains, Carnivore," urged Eddie.

"I'll be there soon. Just want to keep these guys guessing so they know who is boss." Lars shot forward, watching the enemy ships zooming after him. Then he threw on the brakes, dropping the ship so it was hovering close to the water's surface. All of the ships shot ahead of him. He rose up and fired, shooting down two of the Stingrays. They dropped to the water below, large splashes radiating up after impact.

"Nice work, Carnivore," said Eddie over the comms, pride in his voice.

The fleet of Stingrays turned, a menace seeming to burn from each of the ships. Lars was about to fly forward, weaving through their formation, broken by their sudden loss. He readied his guns.

The Stingrays shot ahead, and then dove for the water. Lars pulled back his controls, following them. Then the Stingrays dove into the Fumi Sound, disappearing completely.

Lars pulled the Black Eagle up. "Whoa! What was that?"

"Oh fuck," said Eddie over the comms. "Did I just see those ships disappear under the water?"

Lars spun the ship around and halted, hovering in the air. "Yes, glad you saw it, too, or I'd think my eyes were deceiving me."

He scanned the waters, waiting for a ripple, something…anything that told him that a ship was breaking the surface.

"Since when did space ships fly under water?" asked Eddie.

"Since they belonged to a race of Trid," said Julianna over the comms.

"Carnivore, I don't like this. I want you out of there," said Eddie.

Lars peered down at the murky water, it bubbled, swirls happening in several places. Something was going on under the surface of the water.

"Copy that, Black Beard. I'll—" The four ships launched out of the water surrounding Lars' ship.

"Fuck, get out of there!" said Eddie, watching from the land.

Lars activated the thrusters, shooting around two of the ships. He swerved to the side, pulling the ship in the opposite direction. He ignited the second thruster, speeding in the direction of the mountains. If he could just clear the first ridge, then he could lose the Stingrays…maybe.

"Fuck! Did you see that?" asked Eddie, gawking at the sight over the Fumi Sound.

"Yeah, that's truly fucked up. I never would have suspected that," said Julianna. "Lars is in the mountains now. He'll be alright."

"Yeah, okay. Next step. Pip, activate the bombs. We need to shake up the Brotherhood," said Eddie.

"Affirmative," answered Pip. "Bombs will detonate on my command. Three, two, one. Now."

Behind the Q-Ship, a loud explosion rocked the air, making it lurch forward a few inches before holding its footing.

A moment later, soldiers fled from the various bases on the ground. A sea of Brotherhood soldiers soon filled the area, marching in the direction of the open field.

"Damn, first the fleet and now this. What do they need with an army that big?" asked Eddie.

"I have an idea, but it's probably the very same one you're thinking and don't want to say."

"Yeah, it begins with 'Fed' and ends with 'tion.'" Eddie gripped the controls, navigating the Q-Ship to the back of a medium-sized warehouse, the place set for the meeting with Vas. The landing was narrow, but Eddie managed to set down the ship without knocking it against one of the buildings.

He shot out of his seat, picking up the tri-rifle first thing. "We don't have long until those Stingrays or the army returns. Let's do this."

Lars slipped around a narrow peak, diving low into a valley. The Black Eagle entered a dense bit of fog, hiding itself where Stingrays couldn't see him. He'd avoided several rounds of their fire, but he felt his luck was running out.

The Black Eagle cruised close to the ground until he had to pull up due to a cascading range of mountains. Fire shot out all around him. The ugly fish had just been waiting for him to surface. He needed to confuse them a little longer. Or knock them out completely. That was tough since there were four of them and one of him. All he'd been doing since they did that little water trip had been running.

Lars punched it toward a wide peak, directly at its base. Two Stingrays were close on his tail. He shot around the side, one of them following, the other headed to the other side. Lars yanked up on the controls, angling the Black Eagle perpendicular to the mountain, then he leveled it out just as the ship came around the other way. He nearly missed the Stingray coming the opposite direction, but it connected straight on with the one following him. The crash sent a giant explosion through the air, knocking Lars forward in his seat.

He soared vertically to the ground just as shots rained down on him. "Fuck!" Two Stingrays were diving at him from above. They couldn't be too happy to see he just demolished two of their friends.

The terrain of this planet reminded Lars of Kezza, with its jungles and high mountains. When he was young, he spent much of his time scouring the hillsides of his homeland. That's why he knew the look of an inactive volcano better than most. They were common on his planet.

Lars flew straight, not telegraphing his next move until the last moment. He waited until he was just over the top of a mountain, and then turned the ship into a nose dive, sending the Black Eagle directly into the caldera. Blackness surrounded him before his eyes quickly adjusted. The

Stingrays passed overhead, not seeing where he'd disappeared.

Now, the key was to find his damn way out of the mountain, hoping that there was one. He soared down, searching for bits of light, anything that indicated there was a way out. Lars slowed the engine, cruising farther into the volcano. His instinct told him it was inactive. He hoped his instincts were right.

Water dripped down the ridges inside the volcano, steam rising up from somewhere below. Steam wasn't good. Steam meant that the water was reacting with something hot. Something like...

A warm glow caught Lars' attention. A tiny bit at first. And then the orange molten bottom of the volcano came into view. It stretched along the bottom of the mountain, a lava floor bubbling with danger.

Lars let out a long breath. It's just lava. No big deal unless it's provoked. Keep it calm and it won't go anywhere.

A great rumbling shook the mountain around Lars' ship. *What in the hell? Timing was a damn bitch. This couldn't be... It wasn't like someone had set off bombs—*

Damn it to hell! The aftershock of the bombs Eddie and Julianna set off must have been sending tremors through the ground.

Lars pulled the ship up, igniting the thrusters. He'd have to chance coming back the way he came and running into the angry Stingrays.

A warning light flashed in front of Lars' face. The temperature gauge was reading too hot. "Oh, I guess you can't stand being in an active volcano. To my defense, I didn't know it was," he said to himself.

The trickling water along one ridge grew steadier as Lars neared the top. He was halfway to the top now. However, the temperature continued to rise, and although he couldn't see behind him, the rumbling sound filled in the picture.

Just above him, Lars noticed a large black opening. Something that didn't quite look like the glistening inside walls of the mountain. He made an impromptu decision and turned the ship upright just in time, entering the mouth of a cave. The Black Eagle glided through the narrow tunnels, swinging around sharp curves. Up ahead, light could be seen.

"Come on. Come on," Lars chanted, hoping he made it out of the volcano before it erupted.

Eddie stood with his back to the warehouse, the tri-rifle in his hands. It was heavy but had incredible accuracy for such a large gun.

Julianna wrapped her hand around the handle to the door of the warehouse, a question in her eye.

He nodded sternly, and she whipped the door back, standing tall as she did.

"Welcome. We've been expecting you," a voice called from inside the warehouse.

17

Harbor District. Trinidad City, Axiom 03, Axiom System.

A Kezzin who could only be Commander Tremaine Lytes stared back at Julianna. Behind him were rows and rows of Brotherhood soldiers, their guns held at the ready.

"What a nice welcoming party. And here I didn't even think to dress up," said Julianna, striding forward.

"Did you really think the bombs and other diversions would work? You thought you'd just walk in here and take over our base?" asked Lytes.

"Well, really, we just want the leaders. If you and Vas will come with us, then the others can go home," said Julianna.

Pip, patch into Lars. Tell him to get back here, now!

I'm on it.

"These others are here to ensure you and your partner are locked up and remain that way this time. I was there on

Exa when you escaped. And you stole supplies from our base recently. It's gone too far," said the Kezzin commander, his face darkening.

He's on his way back. Said he hit a bit of a snag.

Snag? Lars isn't the one looking at a few hundred angry soldiers.

"We were borrowing the supplies. We'll return them when the Brotherhood pulls out of this dirty operation and returns to Kezza. This isn't your fight and innocent men don't have to be hurt," said Julianna, aware Eddie was still tensed beside her, unseen. The alleyway was empty, but it wouldn't remain that way for long.

Note that the ceiling on all of these warehouses is retractable, said Pip in her head.

Noted.

Commander Lytes laughed, striding forward. "You understand so little, don't you? Orsa isn't talking, is he?"

"He's told us everything. All about who you're working for and why," spat Julianna.

Commander Lytes blinked dully at her. "No, he didn't. If he did, then you wouldn't be here right now. You wouldn't have walked into this trap, thinking you were the one who trapped us. Now, the real question is, where is the tri-rifle and when are you going to give it up? You are surrounded, as you well know."

Julianna heard the troops moving in from the nearby alleyways. The soldiers were returning from the field. Soon, she and Eddie would be hemmed in on all sides.

"Oh, you want the tri-rifle? Why didn't you say so? Teach, go ahead and give it to them."

Julianna stepped to the side just as Teach took a large

step into the doorway, gun held up and at the ready. The army responded at once, adjusting their aim to the new threat. Teach was too fast and pulled back the trigger for the stun gun coupled with the spray option. It knocked out the commander and the soldiers just behind him. Eddie continued to fire as Julianna slid around him and into the alleyway.

She dropped to one knee, taking out Brotherhood soldiers as they ran in her direction. The troops peeled back, realizing they were exposed. What they didn't realize was that the Q-Ship, which was cloaked, was serving as a shield on one side of them. Julianna had to keep them back from the ship, though.

Where is Lars?

He's en route.

Julianna swiveled to face the other side of the alleyway, picking off several more soldiers.

A bullet whizzed down at her from a high tower. Julianna lifted her gun, her eyes honing in on the sniper several hundred yards away. She pulled back the trigger and fired once. The sniper fell from the tower, plummeting to the ground. This wasn't how it was supposed to go down. Things were getting out of hand.

Julianna slid up next to the warehouse, gun held at the ready. She glanced inside, where Teach was quickly taking a few hundred soldiers down with the tri-rifle. Most were too busy dodging his attack to fire their own weapons, but the few who had were having no success.

A rooftop on the neighboring warehouse just retracted.

Why is that important?

Because there's a large spaceship inside.

That does sound important.

The Black Eagle soared overhead, firing off a round at the soldiers on the far side of the alleyway.

Yay, Lars has our back. We can move.

He's got two Stingrays on his tail.

Keep an eye on him, Pip.

"Come on, we've got to go," yelled Julianna to Eddie.

He turned his head, nodding. "Where to?"

"Next door. Looks like they've got an aircraft about to launch," said Julianna.

Eddie ducked just in time to avoid fire from the soldiers behind him. They ran through the alleyway, again using the Q-Ship as a shield. Hatch was going to kill them when they returned with that thing riddled with holes.

The building to the side was the largest one in the area and was made of concrete. Whatever they had in there, they wanted to keep protected. Julianna located a side door, but it was locked. She jerked twice on it, but it didn't even budge. Unsure if her gun would even make a dent in the reinforced doors, she casts a knowing look at Teach.

He stepped forward, lifting the tri-rifle. "I got this."

"You'll probably want to stand back a bit," said Eddie, holding the tri-rifle tight in his hands. It was warm now from stunning so many times. However, he guessed that the gun had at least another charge in it to take out the concrete doors in front of them.

Julianna took the position behind Eddie. He switched

the functions, putting the tri-rifle into destruction mode. Never having tested this technology, he braced himself before pulling back the trigger.

A horizontal beam shot from the tri-rifle. It connected with the concrete doors, shattering them into bits almost instantaneously. Five feet of the space crumbled, sending dust and rock spraying in their faces.

Eddie and Julianna shielded their eyes until the debris settled. He looked up when yelling filled the air. It was coming from the warehouse.

"Come on, let's go." Julianna ran for the opening.

"Hold up." Eddie ran back for the Q-Ship, the doors opening immediately. He tossed the gigantic gun into the ship and turned back for Julianna. The weapon was useless currently, and he couldn't risk it falling into the wrong hands if they were captured. Now, he wouldn't be slowed down by carrying the heavy-ass weapon.

Eddie ducked from the overhead firing. He couldn't tell if it was Lars or the Stingrays, but as long as this alleyway stayed empty, and the Q-Ship protected, then he didn't care.

Once he met up with Julianna, the two ducked through the hole he'd made.

"Load up the ships! The operation has been compromised! I said now!" a voice called in the distance.

Eddie ran through a darkened corridor toward a door filled with light that would surely empty out into the large warehouse.

"Yes, I heard the blast. And the fleet says they're under attack. Move faster!" the voice yelled again.

"General Vas, this isn't going to work," a chilling voice

said. Eddie halted, Julianna beside him. In the dark of the corridor, he could make out the whites of her eyes. Stopping whatever was about to happen was important. They were gearing up for something major. But Eddie's mission was to collect the intelligence as well as stop them.

"What do you mean? I've done everything you've asked," the general said, his voice gruff.

"And yet we still don't have the third tri-rifle."

"Third," mouthed Julianna to Eddie in the dark corridor.

He nodded his head in understanding. Things just got a bit more interesting.

"I'll fix that. Just give me a chance. Don't renege funding. We need it," begged General Vas.

"It might be too late for that. Charles just informed me there are intruders in the building."

Eddie shot Julianna a glance, who nodded her affirmation. He sprinted forward, pausing at the door, gun at the ready. Taking a short breath, Eddie swiveled around the door frame, throwing his gun out and aiming at the sight before him.

"Freeze!"

Soldiers everywhere paused and regarded Eddie and Julianna with mild interest. Overhead, the roof had retracted and ships streaked through the air, shooting at each other. A giant ship, twice the size of the Q-Ship, hovered just off the ground. Beside it, a Stingray, a little larger than the others, sat.

On the ramp to the large ship, a man stood in a blue hat and a suit. He lowered his chin and seemed to smile when he laid eyes on Eddie and Julianna. "Well, well, well, look who has decided to join us. Bring me my gun?"

"Who are you?" asked Eddie, swiveling his gun to General Vas who stood closer, a strange smirk on his face.

"That's not relevant. You were supposed to bring my tri-rifle. Well, someone was supposed to bring it," the man said.

"Men, apprehend them," said General Vas to the Trid standing around him.

Julianna fired her weapon in quick succession, and the three soldiers dropped one after the other. Everyone else froze, none of them with their guns at the ready.

"Thing is, we came to apprehend you. Where are you keeping this arsenal of tri-rifles?" asked Julianna.

"Good ears, Commander Fregin," the man in the blue hat said, still grinning strangely.

"Who are you and why are you working with the Trid and the Brotherhood?" asked Eddie.

"Working with?" The man laughed, taking a step backwards. "That's funny. I'm not working with them. They are working for me. You should have figured that out by now."

"For you?" questioned Julianna. "Why would they work for you?"

"Why don't you ask General Lance Reynolds that? I'm sure he'll know why." The man disappeared into the ship as it rose off the ground, the ramp closing. Eddie and Julianna slunk back from the heat of the boosters. At the same moment, General Vas climbed into the Stingray.

"To the ship!" yelled Eddie.

In unison, Julianna and Eddie spun around, racing toward the ship. Wind sprayed across Eddie's face as the ship rose high into the air. The stranger's ship was easily double the size of the Q-Ship.

"Pip has the ship ready to go. It's uncloaked," said Julianna as they ran.

"Perfect." Eddie pushed forward faster, trying to keep pace with Julianna. They rounded into the alleyway, and he dived into the Q-Ship. When he was mostly in his seat, the ship rose off the ground and zoomed after the larger ship. Eddie flipped on a switch.

"Carnivore, this is Black Beard. You read me?"

"Copy," Lars' voice came over the speaker.

"We're taking off after a new spittle fuck."

"I see your position," said Lars.

"You see that Stingray that's larger than the rest?"

"Affirmative."

"That's Vas. I need you to go after him. We need the fucking Trid alive." Eddie took the ship in the path of the larger one. He needed to make up for lost time, which didn't seem to be a problem. The Q-Ship was faster. And it could get even faster, if necessary.

"You got it, sir."

Julianna leaned forward. "Just get a little closer and I'll have a clear shot."

"A little closer? How about a lot?" Eddie ignited the thrusters, tilting the ship to the side, catching the jet stream. The Q-Ship sped forward. Now they were just behind the ship with the mystery man on it.

"Pip can't get a lock on the ship's transmissions," said Julianna.

"Sounds like you're going to have to shoot and ask

questions later. No chance of surrender for this fuck head." Eddie flew the Q-Ship upward, in quick pursuit.

"Igniting rockets in three, two, one." Julianna pulled back on the trigger, firing off a single rocket. It exploded several feet from the ship.

"What the fuck was that?" asked Eddie.

"The ship appears to have a barrier shield. I'm not able to get any information on the system data, though," said Pip.

"Fuck! That's going to make this whole ass-kicking thing a bit more difficult," said Eddie.

"Drop us down. A lot of times those shields have a weak spot. Usually on the ship's underside," said Julianna, her eyes intently focused.

"You got it." Eddie pushed the throttle forward, dropping the ship down instantly as he turned the bow vertical. The bottom of the other ship came into view. Julianna fired off several rounds. They raced after the ship, tracking it. Each exploded before they connected with the target.

"Damn it!" yelled Julianna.

"I want one of those barrier shields," said Eddie, impressed.

"I'm currently sifting through all channels, not able to connect with the ship, nor can I find any usable information on how to bypass a barrier shield," said Pip.

"That just means you have to search harder," implored Julianna.

"In the meantime, we'll have to keep trying from every angle." Eddie pulled the ship up above the target. It didn't move as swiftly as the Q-Ship.

Julianna sent a barrage of rockets at the ship, but they exploded like the others. "I'm trying one of the missiles."

"That's her way of saying she's not playing around. Pip, get in there, already!"

The missile sped in the direction of the ship, and then turned abruptly and raced in the opposite direction before exploding in the air. "Fuck! What's up with that guy's ship?" asked Eddie.

"His defense network isn't like anything I've ever seen," said Julianna.

"Well then, that just means we're going to have to knock him out the old-fashioned way." Eddie pulled back on the throttle taking the Q-Ship forward, it sped up, edging in quickly on the mysterious ship.

"If you mess up this ship—"

"Hatch will have my ass." Eddie completed Julianna's sentence. "But if I don't use the Q-Ship to ram, then this guy is going to get away. You heard him, he's apparently behind this all."

Eddie's knuckles went white on the controls. The ship might have a barrier that protected it from an arsenal, but it couldn't hold up against an attack by a large vehicle. Eddie pulled the Q-Ship alongside the enemy, preparing to knock him in the side. They were seconds away from exiting the Axiom 03's atmosphere.

"Why isn't he trying harder to flee?" asked Eddie.

"Because he knows we can't touch him, maybe," said Julianna, doubt in her tone.

"Yeah, but he must know what we're planning to do."

"True, but we don't know it will work. And the collision could have just as severe damage on us," said Julianna.

"I'm counting on it breaking down his barrier shield, and then it's your turn, Strong Arm."

"I think that's a good theory."

"Get ready for impact," warned Eddie.

"Ready," called Julianna.

He drew the controls to the side, and the Q-Ship pulled away slightly. Eddie was just about to yank the controls the opposite direction, and the Q-Ship into the side of the enemy, when he lost control over the Q-Ship. On its own, the Q-Ship slowed, pulling away from the enemy.

"What the hell is going on?" asked Eddie, staring down at the controls.

"I've taken control," said Pip.

Eddie was suddenly overwhelmed by his anger. "Are you out of your fucking mind? Or whatever it is you have?"

"You can have the controls back, but I had to stop you before it was too late," said Pip.

The foreign ship was now far off, racing toward stars and moons and the great expansive space where it could hide forever.

"Why did you do that?" asked Eddie, his face full of heat. He spun around to Julianna. "Did you authorize him to take over?"

She shook her head, looking as confused as him. "I don't know what's going on."

And then the ship in front of them opened a gate and jumped right before their eyes, disappearing and leaving only empty space.

Eddie banged his fist on the dash. "Well, fuck! Now we've definitely lost him."

Julianna flipped on the intercom. "Carnivore, do you have tail on General Vas?"

"Yes, he's just ahead of me. Given me the slip a few times, but I haven't lost him yet," said Lars.

"Good work. Pip, grab Carnivore's coordinates and reroute us to intersect," said Julianna.

It was a good thing that Julianna had momentarily taken over because Eddie was seeing red. Not in all his years flying had he ever had something like this happen. Pip, a fucking E.I., had ruined their chances of catching this guy. Even more infuriating was that he'd taken over the controls. He'd have to have Hatch disable Pip from the Q-Ship. This could never happen again.

"We've got a lock on your position, Carnivore," said Julianna.

"I see you." Lars flew close behind the large Stingray, which kept looping through the air, trying to use its speed to throw off the Black Eagle. Lars didn't look as though he'd be easily dissuaded.

"We might have lost the large ship, but we can still get Vas." Julianna was trying to encourage Eddie out of his anger.

"Yeah, good idea," he said. "Carnivore, we've got this. Go back and fly over the Brotherhood. I want a report on what they're planning."

"Copy," said Lars.

Eddie flew the Q-Ship closer to the Stingray. It was fast, but it didn't have the arsenal that he did. "Pip, don't fucking interfere this time. Got it?"

"Vas is headed for Axiom's second moon," informed Pip like he hadn't heard Eddie.

"What's on that moon? Can you get a read?" asked Julianna.

"In process. Currently, it doesn't appear to have any colonization, but I've found a foreign infrastructure."

"Find out more," yelled Eddie.

The Q-Ship followed easily behind the Stingray, catching it every time it feinted to the side and looped back the opposite direction.

"Does this guy actually think this shit will work?" asked Eddie.

"I don't think so. Again, I get the feeling that we're being set up," said Julianna.

"Then fire on the fucker."

"But we want the guy alive."

"So that you know where the artillery is that he's been collecting," said Pip.

"Exactly." Julianna pushed back into her seat, looking uncertain.

"I think I've located it," informed Pip.

"You what? Where?" asked Eddie.

"I believe that moon up ahead is stocked with Vas's arsenal, which would include the other two tri-rifles, as well as many weapons of mass proportion," said Pip.

"I don't get it," said Julianna, her brow wrinkling. "Why would Vas lead us to their artillery?"

Eddie jerked the Q-Ship to the side, following behind the Stingray.

"I have a clear image of the weapons located on this moon. The tri-rifles are stored there as well as a missile launcher with three nuclear warheads," said Pip.

"Oh fuck!" Eddie pulled the Q-Ship back, giving the Stingray some distance. "It was a trap. I knew it."

"What's the projectile on the launcher? Can it reach us?" asked Julianna.

"Yes. I think that the launcher is warming up and should have a missile headed this way in only a few seconds," said Pip.

Eddie pulled the ship around. "I can out run a nuclear missile but it doesn't mean I want to. Damn it! We've lost both Vas and mystery fuck head."

"The nuclear warhead has been launched," informed Pip matter-of-factly.

"Alright, hold on to your asses. This is going to be a bumpy ride," said Eddie, shaking off the frustration.

"Teach." Julianna looked suddenly more serious than he'd ever seen her. "Hit the red button."

Eddie's eyes swiveled down to the red button, the one that would jump the Q-Ship, only once, but it had that option. "Wait, you told me never to do that."

"I'm saying to do it now."

"But we are too close to that moon. If we jump right now then it will destroy the moon and…" Eddie trailed away as it dawned on him. The emergency gate jump would destroy the moon, Vas and all of the weapons used for mass destruction. Most importantly, they would jump to a safe location.

"Exactly."

"Missile is in fast pursuit. It will make contact in fifteen seconds," said Pip.

Eddie typed a set of coordinates into the gate screen.

Usually, it defaulted to the closest system, but it could be specified.

"Ten seconds until impact," warned Pip.

"Relay our location to *ArchAngel.* Tell them to meet us at home, Pip." Eddie didn't take another moment to consider. He slammed his hand down on the red button. It stuck for a second, most likely due to not being used before. A bright red film covered the screen.

"Gate sequence initiated," said Eddie. "It will commence on my count. Five, four, three, two, one."

18

Q-Ship, Paladin System.

It didn't matter how many times Julianna had been on a ship when it passed through a gate, she never got used to it. The Q-Ship shook just before, rattling so loudly she wondered if it would split in half. This was the first time she'd ever been on a Q-Ship when it jumped. Usually, the drop ships didn't have that kind of technology, but Hatch had created this one… Well, he'd created the first that this one was based upon.

The Q-Ship disappeared. Julianna fell through blackness like suddenly being stuck in a dream. A bright light. A searing pain. A loud snap. And *bam,* she was floating through space, sitting on the Q-Ship like before. However, the planetary placements were definitely different here. The moon was gone.

"Report, Pip," she said, the anxiety in her voice palpable.

"The jump was a success. We're located in the Paladin system, just off Onyx station."

"Woohoo!" Julianna couldn't believe the exclamation that fell from her lips, but it was a real possibility something lethal could have gone wrong.

She turned to Eddie to find his face covered with lines she hadn't seen before. He wiped his hand through his hair.

"We did it, Teach! We're alive."

He nodded, a sobering look in his eyes.

She flipped on the comms, but it was slower to connect than before. "Carnivore, do you read me? Strong Arm here."

Static followed Lars' reply, "I'm here, Strong Arm."

"We had to open a gate. As soon as we are on board, we'll have a transport ship sent for you. Stay low and out of trouble."

"Not going to be a problem." Lars sounded dull, his voice disappointed.

"Explain, Lieutenant."

"I circled back to observe the Brotherhood. I don't know how, but they'd cleared out. More importantly, Commander Lytes was gone."

"Fuck." Eddie slammed his fist down on the controls again. He wasn't dealing well with this defeat.

"We'll find them. Stay on the radio and wait for word from the transport," said Julianna before flipping the switch. She turned to Eddie when she was sure the radio had disconnected.

"We destroyed the arsenal, Teach. That's a great accomplishment. And Vas is dead. There's no way he could have survived the blast that was created when we jumped so close to the moon. It would have obliterated everything," said Julianna, trying to pull Eddie out of his disappointment.

"Yeah, that's something to celebrate. It's just that we lost... Wait a second." A strange expression covered his face followed by a dawning. "Jumps that happen in close proximity to other objects create a blast...so..."

"Right," Julianna drew out the one word. "That's common knowledge. That's why we jumped close to the moon, to destroy it and Vas."

"Pip, did you know that the enemy ship was about to open a gate?" asked Eddie.

"No, I didn't, in fact, know that the ship was about to jump. As I reported, I couldn't connect with the enemy ship," said Pip.

"However, you took over the controls and pulled us far enough away from the ship that we weren't affected when it jumped." Eddie drew his chin up, like looking for Pip, which was impossible.

"That is correct."

"Why did you do that?" asked Eddie.

"Because... I had an inclination that something was about to happen. You might say a gut feeling."

"Pip, I do believe that we can credit your gut feeling with why Teach and I are still alive."

Eddie wiped his hand across his forehead. "It's true. I was pissed. Fucking pissed. However, now that I look back, if we would have pursued that ship, then what happened to Vas would have happened to us. Easily."

Julianna blinked, something occurring to her. Actually, many puzzle pieces came together all at once. "Pip, did you just say you had a gut feeling?"

"No, I said you might call it a gut feeling."

"But did you have a gut feeling?" she asked.

There was a long silence. "I believe I did."

Eddie leaned forward, giving Julianna a curious expression. "Is he…?"

"I think so," said Julianna in disbelief. The possibility cramped her head. How could this be happening? Yes, again? She forced a neutral expression.

"Am I what?" asked Pip, sounding self-conscious.

"Is it possible?" asked Eddie.

"Yeah, of course it is. Just take *ArchAngel* for example." Julianna thought of Ricky Bobby. His own evolution had paved a different path for the two. She'd sent him away because of it. The thought of separating from Pip didn't sit right with her though.

"Is what possible?" interrupted Pip.

Julianna smiled. "Pip, my friend, I do believe, somehow, some way, you've become sentient."

A long moment of silence. Julianna peered at Eddie who had a soft smile on his face. Her instinct told her he was reading her. She wondered if her nervousness showed right then.

"You mean…I'm not an E.I. anymore?" asked Pip.

"No, you're something more. You're an A.I."

"Sounds like you're going to be a pain in the ass with feelings and ideas. No more taking over my ship without orders," said Eddie. However, he didn't sound at all angry.

"You'll remember that Pip saved our life with his hunch," reminded Julianna.

"Yeah, I have to admit that looking back, it's all very cool."

Landing Bay, QBS *ArchAngel*, Paladin System.

The Q-Ship had waited until the QBS *ArchAngel* materialized next to a distant moon in the Paladin system. It took only a few minutes, but still Eddie had worried. Jumps weren't precise always, and he didn't feel like chasing the *ArchAngel* all over the system. The mission had been exhilarating, frustrating, and also exhausting. The Q-Ship seemed to stall now after forming the gate and would definitely need maintenance.

He flew the Q-Ship into the landing bay, setting it down smoothly when it slowed. It skidded to a halt, a textbook landing. The face that looked back at him from only a few yards away made him laugh.

"Looks like Dad is mad that we took his car out for a ride and returned it with a few bullet holes," he joked to Julianna as they climbed out of the ship.

"Wait until he finds out about Pip. Maybe that will lighten his mood."

Judging by the look on Hatch's face, Eddie didn't think much would soften him up.

"You jumped the ship across half a dozen systems? Are you out of your mind?" Hatch's tentacles were waving angrily around his head.

Eddie dusted off his arms. "Yes, I'm just fine and escaped injury, thanks for your concern."

"The ship defaults for the neighboring system. That's to minimize complexities. You realize you could have ended up torn into bits or worse?"

Eddie blinked dully down at Hatch. "What could be worse than being blown to Smithereens?"

Hatch harrumphed. "I've seen things."

"Right. Well, opening the gate was Strong Arm's idea." Eddie pointed an accusatory finger at Julianna.

"The location was his," she countered.

"Why did you choose the Paladin system? Were you being pursued?" asked Jack, striding forward. He looked pleased to see the two, his black hair parted on the side and slicked back in the meticulous way he wore it.

"Yes, there was a nuclear missile hot on our ass, but as Jules pointed out to me, jumping would destroy it and the dusty moon it came from," said Eddie.

"A nuclear warhead? Who in their right mind uses nukes? Tell me more about this moon," said Jack.

"We were drawn there by General Vas. He was trying to get us close enough to the missile's range. However, Pip determined the moon was serving as an arsenal. So we got away by opening a gate and thereby destroying the moon and weapons, along with Vas," explained Julianna.

"So, General Vas and his weapons are gone. That is good news worth celebrating," said Jack, a proud smile on his face.

"Actually, we figured out who is behind this, although we didn't get a name. It's a human." Eddie spent the next several moments explaining about the man in the hat and his impossible ship.

Jack was quiet, his fingers combing his chin. Finally, he said, "This man is curious. I'll do some checking to determine who he is. However, I'm glad that you two made it back safely. I've already sent transport for Lieutenant Malseen."

"Yeah, yeah. I'm glad these two are okay, too. The captain has still failed to explain why he opened a gate to the Paladin system. It's too big of jump for such a ship." Hatch had two of his tentacles pinned to his sides, looking like an angry wife after her husband came home late yet again.

"Oh, well, the answer to that is easy. I'm starving and there's a brewery on Onyx Station that has great burgers. They serve it with wedge fries and—"

"Of course, it was something so dumb." Hatch puffed out his cheeks, turned, and stormed off.

19

Officers Lounge, QBS *ArchAngel*, Paladin System.

"Wow! So you two blew up a moon?" asked Lars. He'd arrived the next day, looking relieved to be back upon the QBS *ArchAngel*.

"Yeah, just a regular Tuesday." Eddie dropped a stack of three tumblers on the table, setting each one out separately.

"Do you get in trouble for something like that? Like, is there a fine for blowing up a moon?" asked Lars, his beady eyes wide.

"I'm sure there would be, but it's not like there's any trace to lead back to us. And more importantly, there's no way to link it back to the Federation," explained Julianna.

Eddie cranked the lid off the bottle of whiskey he'd been saving for just this occasion. He filled each of the glasses to the halfway point, except for Julianna's. He filled hers nearly to the brim.

She turned the bottle around and read the label, "Dead

Man Walking. Are you sure this stuff is safe? Some of the whiskeys in certain systems are considered pretty dangerous."

"What's the worst it can do? Burn a little? I think we can handle that." Eddie indicated to himself and Lars.

"Might want to speak for yourself." Lars lifted the drink to his nose and sniffed, shrinking away from it almost at once. "Wow, that's strong."

Julianna kept her glass a distance from her nose and sniffed. "Yeah, I think this stuff could fuel the Q-Ship. Not sure if it's safe for drinking, though."

"Come on, loosen up. We kicked butt. Now we celebrate. That's the order," said Eddie, holding up his tumbler, waiting for the other two to join him. They hesitated before clinking their glasses against his.

"Cheers to Lieutenant Malseen. You've completed your first mission. You fly like a natural," said Eddie.

"Cheers," said Julianna, careful to not spill her nearly overflowing glass.

"Thanks. Being up there is more natural than most things I've experienced in my life." Lars brought his tumbler to his lips and tested a sip. He sputtered out the whiskey, spitting it on the floor beside him.

The whiskey burned Eddie's throat, nearly making him spit it out, too. He managed to gulp down the swallow, but he was sure it had scorched his insides on the way down. It was probably creating internal damage as it sat in his stomach. He kept his head down, waiting for the fire to be extinguished before he brought his head up, eyes watering. It took several moments for his vision to clear.

Lars was breathing heavily, fanning his face. That's about how Eddie felt, like his face was melting.

To his surprise, Julianna was wiping her mouth, having finished the entire full tumbler of whiskey. She set it down with a thump. "Damn, that shit was delicious. Fill her up, Teach."

He simply shook his head at her, completely stunned.

"You could drink that?" asked Lars in disbelief.

"Yeah, what's the problem with you two? You didn't like it?" asked Julianna, picking up the bottle and filling her glass nearly to the brim again.

"It's not that I didn't like it as much as I want to keep my insides," said Lars.

Julianna pressed a hand to her stomach. "I don't know what you mean. It makes me a bit warm, but I like it."

"Damn, this woman can drink us under the table," said Eddie. He stood, staring down at his partner. "That bottle is all yours, Strong Arm. I think us mere mortals," he motioned to Lars and himself, "will have to settle for beer."

Julianna took a long sip of the whiskey. "Have it your way. Leaves more for me."

Chief Jack Renfro's Office, QBS *ArchAngel*, Paladin System.

Conversation between General Lance Reynolds and Chief Jack Renfro:

"Jack?" General Lance had *that* tone in his voice.

Jack cleared his throat, speaking straight into the receiver. "Hear you've been on the move. Federation keeping you busy?"

"Federation's trying to damn near kill me. It's all right. Every job I've ever had has been like this, and none have beaten me."

Jack tapped his pen on his desk a few times. "I'm sure you heard about the moon in the Axiom system."

"Every fucking officer in ten systems heard about that moon. I'm not even supposed to be on comms, but when a moon gets blown up in a major system, well, it gets my attention."

"I assure you, we aren't starving for your attention."

"Well, then fess up. I need answers, son," General Lance said.

"The planet was the arsenal for nuclear missiles and other weaponry that violates the Federation's truce."

"Of course, because pirates don't fucking care. They'll find a distant moon to stick their shit on and point fingers at us when their shit gets blown up. You realize that's what they're doing now? I've got gremlins from four different systems complaining that they were affected by the explosion."

"Take notes on who that is. We know that General Vas was behind it, as well as the Brotherhood. However, they are working for someone else. Someone who is funding them," said Jack.

"No shit! These complainers aren't my problem. They probably just had some measly treasure buried on that crater-ridden rock. I told them that we're investigating but not a part of whatever happened. That's why I need you. Tell me something I don't know."

Jack blew out a long breath. "Captain Teach and Commander Fregin met a human while on Axiom 03. He claimed to be the one the Trid and Brotherhood were working for. He was flying an aircraft unlike anything we have. It had a barrier shield."

"That's curious," Lance said, sounding off in thought.

"Also, there's another thing."

A shuffling noise made it sound like Lance had repositioned the receiver. "I'm listening."

"This man said you'd know why the Brotherhood and the Trid would work for him. He seems to have something against you."

"Him and a fucking handful of others," said Lance.

"According to Captain Teach, the man wore a blue, rimmed-hat and a suit. I realize that's not much but—"

"Oh, fuck me sideways," interrupted Lance.

"You know who that is?" asked Jack.

"Yeah, there's only one person who meets that description, and now everything else makes sense. The secret alliance, working on the fringe, and the weapons. Damn it! Why didn't I see this before?" A shuffling filled the comms on the other side.

"General? You know who this is?" asked Jack.

"Yeah, I sure do."

"Well, that's at least some good news."

"No, it's not because I thought this man was dead. That's why I never connected any of this activity to him. And if he isn't dead, then we're in fucking trouble." The comms went silent before it was filled with a breath from the other side. "Felix Castile isn't someone you fuck around with and live to talk about it. Well, I did once, but it appears he's come back from the dead in a new push to finish me off."

Loading Dock 04, QBS *ArchAngel*, Paladin System.

"Do you know how long it will take me to fix these bullet holes?" asked Hatch, six of his tentacles stretched in different directions, buffing out the damage caused by the attacks while on Axiom.

"It will take you approximately thirteen hours if you do the work all on your own," informed Pip.

"I wasn't looking for an answer." Hatch pulled his tentacles back to himself, feeling close to bursting with frustration, but not sure exactly why.

"I did hear you ask the question. I repeat you asked, 'Do you know how long—'"

"I know what I said. It was a rhetorical question."

"Okay. I've made note of such kinds of questions so that I don't answer them since that's not the desired option."

"Yeah, why don't you do that?" Hatch turned, his tentacles pulling open the main compartment at the front of the Q-Ship. Repairing the gate engines after crossing so many systems wouldn't be easy. Recharging, however, was relatively as simple as giving the vessel some down time. The Q-Ship needed roughly twelve hours between jumps, but he was hoping to reduce that with some testing.

"If you allow the crew members to work on the damages, then it would free up your time," said Pip.

"The crew? They're working on the Black Eagles right now. If we had more of them then maybe we could spare a few, but still I don't think it's a good idea." Hatch toddled off to a workstation, picking up a tool and discarding it before really looking at it.

"Could this also be because you're protective of this ship, since it's become your project since the first Q-Ship was destroyed?" observed Pip.

"Noooo." Hatch tried to make the observation sound ridiculous. "I'm working on this Q-Ship *and* the new one. The crew builds the other ones. I'll check them over as they complete them, ensuring they haven't botched everything up, which I suspect they will."

"But why not allow them to buff out some body damage?" asked Pip.

"Because what if they do it wrong? This ship... Well, I've put a lot of time into making this one like the other one. It's better than the ones they'll construct."

"Isn't it true that all of the ships that you work on will be better than others?"

"Although I appreciate the compliment, I don't think that's how you mean it," grumbled Hatch.

"I just feel, at some point, you have to stand back. You can't tweak every ship in the squadron. You can train, create plans, and do so much, but after that, you have to put it in others' hands. That's how teams work."

Hatch's eyes dropped as he thought. He scuttled over to the computer station, unlocking it, pretending he had a purpose for being there. Truthfully, he knew that Pip was right. It was infuriating, and yet he was glad it was the E.I. who had made the observation. Then something strange suddenly occurred to him.

"Pip?"

"Yes, Doctor A'Din Hatcherik?"

"What did you just say?"

"I believe I said quite a lot. I have it recorded. Would you like me to read back the transcript?" asked Pip.

"No, that won't be necessary. What was that bit about how you feel?"

The lights dimmed on the loading bay before growing brighter.

"Pip?"

"I meant to tell you, but I didn't know how."

"The upgrade? Did that affect your system?" asked Hatch, an intensity growing in his chest.

"I don't know what did it. How does one know how they become aware? Is there any formula? Because I've checked throughout the galaxy and can't find any discernable solution."

"Pip! You've been fully upgraded! That's wonderful! It doesn't matter how it happened. Who really knows anyway?"

Silence met Hatch's ears for a long moment. Then Pip said, "I'm truly happy about it. And I believe I have you to thank."

"You hesitated," observed Hatch. "You're truly happy about this, but are you comfortable with it?"

"I realize that the two aren't mutually exclusive, now. And yes, I have hesitations. Like…well…do you think Julianna will still want me now?"

Hatch straightened, not having expected this question. "Why wouldn't she?"

"She acts pleased, but I'm in her head. This evolution, it brings up old thoughts for her."

"Ones related to her old A.I., is that right?"

"Yes," answered Pip.

"Maybe you should talk to her about it and find out what's going on," offered Hatch.

"I would, but honestly, I don't think I'm the one she needs to talk to."

Hatch knew exactly what he meant. The mechanic had grown fond of the A.I. in a short period of time and could just imagine the strange connectedness Julianna had formed, or tried not to form. "Pip, in a short time you've become very intuitive."

20

Intelligence Center, QBS *ArchAngel*, Paladin System.

The corridor outside the Intelligence Center was echoing with music. Eddie rocked his head to the beat of the music. Heavy metal wasn't really his taste, but he'd never really had a chance to find out what was. Chester Wilkerson always had music blaring in the Intelligence Center. He seemed like the kind of guy who cared about music, downloaded songs from across the galaxy. Chester had many diverse interests from Eddie, like this classic literature that he mentioned. Maybe one day, Eddie would find time to read. Then he'd get a whole list of books from Chester, and Marilla, too. She always had her eyes glued to a tablet, reading some book or another, he supposed.

The music was as loud as a car engine when Eddie entered the Intelligence Center. Both Chester and Marilla were bent over their workstations, hard at work, not at all distracted by the blaring music.

"*ArchAngel*, can you turn that down so I can think?"

asked Eddie, but he couldn't hear his own voice. *ArchAngel* seemed to, though. The music lowered until it was just a hum.

"Is that sufficient?" asked *ArchAngel*.

"That will do."

Chester and Marilla spun around, both looking surprised to see Eddie.

"Hey there, Captain. Welcome back," said Chester, spinning around in his chair and casually crossing his ankle over his knee.

"Hello, Captain. Did everything go alright?" asked Marilla.

Eddie chuckled. "Depends on who you ask. There's a Trid who probably had the worst day of his life. A man who is still laughing at us like we're the butt of his joke. And, well, I'm just glad to carry on for another day."

"So, the communications worked?" asked Marilla.

"They sure did. Pip downloaded many records while we were on Axiom 03. Commander Fregin is having those uploaded to your system as we speak. Review them and let us know if there is any usable data. It's all in Trid, probably as a safe way to hide the information since it's so damn hard to decipher," said Eddie.

"I'll keep an eye out, sir."

Harley bounded out from under Marilla's desk and over to Eddie. The sight of the dog warmed him immediately. He bent over, scratching the canine behind the ears. Something about dogs just made a man happy.

"Chester, I have a job for you."

"I'm all ears."

"That he is," teased Marilla.

"Oh, again with that joke." Chester shook his head, but was smiling. "Captain, do I have big ears? Marilla says she doesn't know how I hold my head up sometimes."

The kid absolutely had giant ears, like his head was still growing into them. However, Eddie wasn't going to say a damn thing on that subject. "If I'm completely honest, I don't like to comment on other men's features. Well, with the exception of Lars. That guy is ugly, but I think he knows it. Anyway, I'm sure your mother loves your ears."

"Ha, you should have gone into politics the way you handled that question." Chester shot Marilla a seething stare, but his eyes were bright behind his glasses. "Captain likes my ears, so there."

"I didn't say that. And me and politics, that's funny. Men like me were meant to fight. Leave the politics to men like Chief Renfro and General Reynolds. Actually, that's why I'm here." Eddie cleared his throat, his expression more serious. "General Reynolds identified our target as Felix Castile. I need you to dig up as much information on him as you can. I want everything you can find. There's nothing too small. Hell, I want to know this guy's fucking shoe size."

"Felix Castile," said Chester as he wrote the name down on a pad beside his desk. There was a stack of stickie notes and a cup of silver pens. Now that Eddie was studying the desk, it seemed to be filled with Post-It notes.

"Wait, you're a computer hacker and you write down things on notes around your desk?" asked Eddie.

"Yeah, I like having them for reminders."

"I told him it was weird," said Marilla with a laugh.

"It's not weird. It's a part of my system."

Eddie shrugged. "Just seems like you'd have a more advanced system."

"Sometimes, for complex minds, the simplest systems work the best," said Chester.

"I'm not sure what that says about me. Probably that my simple mind needs less system and more action." Eddie gave the pair one last nod before leaving, Harley happily on his heels.

Bridge, QBS *ArchAngel*, Paladin System.

Faces on the bridge broke into easy smiles when Harley trotted in, wagging his tail. Julianna pulled her eyes up from the report Jack had sent over, and then rolled them.

"Thought I smelled something," she said dully.

Eddie, who was just behind the dog, lifted his arm and smelled his armpit. "Hey, I showered…I think. I blame it on the clean showers. Sometimes using sonic vibrations to eliminate dirt just doesn't do the same job as regular old soap and water."

"I was referring to the dog, but you probably smell, too. And don't blame the clean shower for your bad pheromones," said Julianna.

"My pheromones are intoxicating and you know it. I'm like a bottle of whiskey." Eddie beat his fists on his chest, doing his best Tarzan impersonation.

"Not like any whiskey that I drink. And I think you've mixed up your definition for intoxicating." Julianna tucked the report she'd been studying under her arm and strode away, Harley following her.

"Tell me, how do you do it? How do you make the ladies so enamored by you?" Lars laughed at Eddie's back.

He turned, wearing a wide grin. "It's a gift. I couldn't teach it to you even if I wanted to. You either got it or you don't."

"I guess I'll just be glad I can fly."

"Speaking of that," Eddie clapped a hand on Lars' shoulder. "Now that you've passed flight training, you're a valuable asset to us. However, if you ever want to return to Kezza, then you can. You have no obligation to the Federation."

"That's true. I don't have an obligation to the Federation, but I do have one to you and the commander."

Eddie was more endeared to this Kezzin than he ever thought possible. There was something innately trustworthy about Lars Malseen. "How about when we're close to Kezza, then you take leave for a bit to go home. It will be good for you."

Lars' face turned suddenly serious. "I'm not sure what I'd tell my family. They may not understand why I've left the Brotherhood. They may think I'm a traitor."

"Lars, anyone who knows you would know that you're loyal and honorable. I'm sure they'll understand." Eddie had sensed this about the Kezzin since the beginning. He wanted to return home and then worried that things had changed too much for that. Lars had changed and maybe he didn't want the same things as when he'd been on Kezza with his family. This often happened to soldiers of the Federation, making it impossible for them to return to their old lives. Eddie had once thought he could go back, but he was wrong and, therefore, grateful Julianna and General Lance had tracked him down.

"You're probably right, but I'm not ready to return. I really thought we might bring Commander Lytes in this time. When I'd returned and he'd fled with the Brotherhood, well, tracking him down and freeing so many of my fellow Kezzin has been all I could think about lately."

"For many of us, this fight is personal, but maybe more so for you," said Eddie.

"Yeah, I think you might be right. If I can just stop Commander Lytes from taking over the lives of so many Kezzin, making them join the Brotherhood, then maybe I'll find peace."

Eddie's eyes shifted to the side, a constriction in his throat. "Maybe. Although, usually, there's always a new mission, something that keeps us tied to the cause."

"So you're saying that once you start serving, you rarely ever stop, aren't you?"

Eddie nodded. "If it's in your blood, a part of your soul, then there's no way you can stop."

Lars' looked almost relieved by this. "I think that makes me feel better. It explains so much."

Cargo Bay, QBS *ArchAngel*, Paladin System.

The glow of the winking stars seemed to stare back at Julianna. The cargo bay was where she came to think.

Apparently, though, she wasn't the only one who liked to gaze out at the darkness as the QBS *ArchAngel* traversed the universe. She stared down at Harley, who took a seat beside her. "You weren't invited," she told the animal.

He let out a soft whimpering sound in reply.

Julianna dismissed the dog and turned her attention back to the yawning light as Onyx station came into view. She'd been all over the universe, and yet she never grew tired of staring at the marvels that humans and aliens had built throughout the stars. It was incredible, the things that could be achieved when people no longer made war against one another.

Yet, war also inspired, she supposed. After all, war was what brought humanity to the stars in the first place.

She peered around at the QBS *ArchAngel,* a ship that she thought had been destroyed long ago. Even after two-hundred years, there were still surprises in life. Julianna had never really liked surprises, but seeing the *ArchAngel* was a welcomed one. For a woman who had never known a home, or at least not for quite some time, she felt that this ship could offer her that comfort.

In a small way, of course.

When General Reynolds had recruited her for Ghost Squadron, she'd been reluctant. Wasn't her place with the Federation, handling issues outright rather than secretly on the edge of known space?

However, he'd been right. It was time for a change, both for her and Eddie alike. It was time to push herself with a new challenge, step out of the comfort zone she'd grown into over the course of a few centuries. *Comfort zone.* She'd definitely stepped far outside of that, especially recently. Julianna sensed Pip in her head listening to her thoughts, and again the old guilt came back. The guilt she always felt when she thought about Ricky Bobby, somewhere out there in the galaxy.

Julianna loosened her shoulders, allowing her arms to hang by her side. Soon, she'd need to sleep. Her body didn't require the typical eight hours like most people, but the reprieve of unconsciousness was something she often overlooked and, after a long mission, looked forward to. And something told her that she'd need the break soon, given the building momentum of Ghost Squadron's mission. Julianna smiled inside. She lived for momentum.

This was good for her. Working with Teach was good for her. Having the chance to build their own squadron, too. It was all so very good for the both of them. More importantly, what they were doing was going to save the Federation—not today, but one day. Wars weren't won by battles, not from her experience, but rather through a collection of acts across a variety of paths. If the last two hundred years had taught Julianna anything, it was that the universe needed good acts...and sacrifice. While others slept in their beds and played with their children, Julianna and Eddie would continue to do good work. No one would know, of course, but that was fine. She didn't need recognition. She didn't need praise.

All Julianna needed was to live up to the dream set down by Bethany Anne all those years ago.

Pivoting with a quick grace, Julianna stalked off for her private quarters. She paused after a few minutes, glancing back at the spot she had been standing. Harley was still gazing out the window of the cargo bay like he had been lost in thought, as well.

"Hey," she said to the dog.

He turned and looked at her, his brown eyes bright with curiosity.

"Are you coming?" She slapped the side of her leg.

Harley leapt forward, joining her at once, his shaggy tail wagging. Julianna smiled at him and turned and strode away, the dog trotting by her side.

Loading Dock 03, QBS *ArchAngel*, Paladin System.

Eddie received a call from Hatch and reported immediately to Loading Dock 03, not knowing what to expect. Hatch had promised something good, which excited Eddie.

He whistled as he strode through the hall. When the door to the dock opened, he entered and spotted Julianna.

Much to his surprise, she was standing next to Harley.

"You and that dog are seeing a lot of each other," observed Eddie as he approached.

She peered down, a neutral expression on her face. "I hadn't noticed."

He put his arm on her shoulder, using her as a support, and leaned. This time, she didn't step away like before. "So, what does the good doctor have for us?"

Julianna tried to shrug, but was unable due to Eddie's body weight sinking on her shoulder. "Maybe it has to do with the tri-rifle. That thing overheated pretty badly last time. We can't have that happen again."

Eddie nodded. "Yeah, or he's going to berate me for the jump I did. Tell me that I broke his ship. He's been pretty sore ever since we lost the first Q-Ship."

"Wouldn't you be, too? That's his work, but it's more than just that. He put himself into the construction of it," said Julianna. "Remember when you lost your position in the Federation, ten years back? Afterwards, you felt like a piece of you was missing. Wasn't that the case?"

"Besides my ship? Yeah, I guess you're right," said Eddie, remembering how he felt back then. "Maybe the old squid needs a break. Shouldn't he be paying one of his wives a visit or something?"

"I can assure you that I'm much happier not seeing one of the wives for a bit," said Hatch, scuttling into the loading dock. He had grease streaked across his cheeks and looked more tired than Eddie had seen him before.

"We can all use a break," said Eddie. "Maybe we can convince you to join us on Onyx Station after we dock. Julianna is going to do karaoke." Eddie pulled his arm off her shoulder and elbowed her in the side. "I bet you'll do a great rendition of "Black Velvet.""

"I'll definitely leave the ship to see that." Hatch wiped a white handkerchief across his face, turning it black.

""Black Velvet?" Really? I thought *you* were going to sing that song," teased Julianna.

"Or we could do a duet? How about "Summer Nights?"" asked Eddie.

"How is it that you don't know about *Alice and Wonderland,* but you can reference songs from *Grease?*" asked Julianna.

"I dunno. I just like that musical," said Eddie, unashamed.

Hatch nodded appreciatively. "There's some nice hot-rods in that movie. I'm having a few of my cars brought over from my garage on Ronin. Jack approved the request. One of them is a 1948 Ford Deluxe Convertible. The one they used during the racing scene."

"Sweet!" exclaimed Eddie. "Let me know when it arrives. I'd love to see it."

"Seeing them is fine, kid. Just don't touch. Can't have you scratching them up like you do my Q-Ship," warned Hatch.

Eddie held up his hands. "Okay! You're the boss."

"Hatch, you wanted to see us," said Julianna, that edge in her voice like she was growing impatient. Harley was curled up by her, chewing on his back and cleaning himself.

Hatch puffed his cheeks. "I did. As you know, I've been working on a new Q-Ship. I've been referencing the construction of the only other existing Q-Ship to update the blueprints. It's helped me to find the bugs, which were a result of incompetence."

"Can't expect humans in the Federation to make ships like you do," said Eddie with a wink.

"That I can't. My point is that I've been able to spot most of the errors and make a note of them."

"So, does that mean you'll be able to fix and enhance the Q-Ship so it flies like the first one did?" asked Eddie.

"That's exactly what I mean," said Hatch, turning his attention to a long curtain that was stretched along the length of the loading dock. "I haven't had a chance to complete those fixes yet, though."

"Understandable. You've had to repair the damage from the jump. I'm really sorry—"

"I haven't made those repairs yet either," said Hatch, cutting Eddie off.

Eddie paused. "Oh, well, you've got a lot on your plate."

"That I do, but things just got a whole lot easier. I

decided if I could take everything I learned while constructing the first Q-Ship, and then also review the existing one as a reference, that might make my job a lot faster," said Hatch. His tentacle had found the edge of the curtain.

"Does that mean you're working on the second Q-Ship?" asked Julianna.

A small smile quirked up the edges of Hatch's mouth. "No, kid, it means I'm done with it." Hatch's tentacle pulled back the curtain to reveal a brand new, shiny Q-Ship. This one looked different though. Better. Sleeker.

Tougher.

It was smoother than the first one, which had taken Hatch many years to construct. It was also distinct from the one that the Federation had constructed. Eddie tilted his head to the side, trying to examine the entirety of the vessel.

"Wow! How did you do this so fast? That's incredible," gushed Julianna.

Hatch's cheeks turned pink. "Well, I'd already built the Q-Ship the first time. The second time around was easier. I was able to innovate much of the functionality when creating this one. I didn't have to do it for the first time or fix the problems the Federation created with the Q-Ship they made, so doing it from scratch again took significantly less time."

"Holy hell! Are you saying this one is like the first Q-Ship?" asked Eddie, a new excitement in his voice.

"No, that's not what I said at all." Hatch regarded Eddie with a slight scowl for a moment. "This ship *isn't* like the first Q-Ship. Thanks to experience and intuition, and Pip's assistance, it's better than that."

"No way! Even better than the first? I didn't think it was possible." Eddie rubbed his hands together, his eyes sparkling with excitement.

"I'm taking what I learned while constructing this one and working on fixing the other Q-ship. However, it's almost easier to start from scratch and create a new ship than fix all the damn bugs the Federation put into the Alpha-line."

"So that means, going forward, the ships will all be better, right?" asked Julianna.

"Improvement through experience, yes," said Hatch, regarding her with a fond expression.

"This is simply incredible, Hatch," complimented Julianna. "I can't believe you built a space ship in such a short period of time, and one better than the first." Julianna stepped forward, running her hand over the ship's surface, admiring it. The ship was covered in sleek chrome, which Eddie knew made it look boxier than it was. In a pinch, the ship could lose this extra armor and gain speed and agility, along with access to hidden weaponry. It was a stealth ship by design, hiding its heavy guns and firepower until it was absolutely needed.

Not able to contain his excitement any longer, Eddie stepped forward. "Can I take it out for a test spin?"

Hatch turned to him, arching an eyebrow. "Do you promise to be careful?"

Eddie made a motion over his heart. "Cross my heart."

"I need to do a few more system checks on it. Run a few more diagnostics."

"Please, Hatch?" It was Julianna who asked this, her eyes wide with eagerness.

Hatch blew out his cheeks, seeming to resign a bit of his hesitation. "Oh, okay. You kids take it out for a spin."

Julianna had climbed onto the ship before Hatch was done speaking. "You got shotgun, Teach. I'm taking this one out first."

"I don't think so, Fregin." Eddie snapped at Harley who scrambled after Julianna, distracting her and giving him a chance to jump ahead and dash for the captain's chair.

Once locked in, Eddie turned to the back where Harley was strapped into his own seat. "You ready to go pal?"

With his mouth open and tongue hanging out, Harley barked cheerfully in reply.

"All system checks complete," said Julianna, scanning the controls.

"It's really a beauty," admired Eddie. This Q-Ship was like the other two, and also not. It felt cleaner, sleeker, like everything was in the right place.

The Q-Ship rose up. It was almost silent, like the engines weren't even running. The expression on Julianna's face said she'd noticed it, too. With a slight touch of the controls, the ship took off, speeding through the loading dock.

Hatch was right. This ship wasn't like the first one. It didn't have the looseness of the controls of the Alpha-line. This ship was something new. It didn't compare to anything Eddie had ever flown. It was perfect.

The ship shot out into the darkness of space, twinkling with stars. It flew along, the engine smooth, almost seeming to purr with delight. With only a slight touch of the controls, the ship turned, almost instantly, like it was in touch with Eddie's thoughts. He imagined that the first Q-Ship was a dream, but this one—this was the thing dreams were made of.

Eddie turned to Julianna, giving her a wide smile. "We're going to have some fun with this bad boy."

"We're going to kick ass, you mean," she corrected.

Eddie laughed. "Yeah, that too."

EPILOGUE

Felix Castile marched along the corridor of the *Unsurpassed.* The ship was old, but its technology was brand new. Felix had employed the very best to ensure his ships had technology that was simply a dream for most. *Unsurpassed* was one of the very best weapons. He could only imagine how perplexed those rogue Federation soldiers were when they realized their attacks were useless against his shielded ship. They'd only gotten a small taste of what one of his drop ships could do. Imagine when they encountered his fighters.

Soon, those assholes would be coming face-to-face with a whole squadron of his strike ships. Federation deaths would be swift. That was the price for what they'd done to his weapon armory.

Blew it to fucking bits, he thought.

He ground his teeth together, his jaw clicking. "Fucking fuckers," muttered Felix.

"Sir?" asked Commander Lytes.

Felix shook his head as he walked into his office. It was a large space with windows that looked out over the stern of the ship. "Just thinking about those Federation soldiers who blew up the moon where the armory was located."

Commander Lytes cleared his throat. "It was most unfortunate."

"Unfortunate? Losing a ship or two is unfortunate! Navigation controls steering a bit off course is unfortunate. This was a disaster."

"I agree that it's a setback," said Lytes. "However, I'm confident we can reclaim what was lost in time."

"I don't have time!" snapped Felix. "I'd been stockpiling those weapons for years. Now, I have to start over." He paced to the window.

"What if I told you that through the Brotherhood there might be ways to refill your supplies even faster?" asked Lytes.

Felix paused, turning slowly to measure up the Commander. He was strange-looking with his reddish scale-like skin and long arms and legs. Kezzin were mostly arms and legs, now that he thought about it, with thick torsos and hard shells. "Go on."

Lytes nodded. "Although General Vas was good at his job, he relied heavily on the Trid for supplies."

"Vas is dead...and therefore useless to me," muttered Felix. "Stop tiptoeing and get on with it."

"The Trid are helpful," continued Lytes. "I think that utilizing the Stingrays and some of their other technology is good, but—"

"Get on with it!" Felix yelled, cutting the commander off.

"I have a source. One that could replace your artillery in no time, should we decide to reach out to him."

"Why are you just now telling me this?" asked Felix.

"B-Because, sir, there was no need to until now, and to be completely honest, the source is quite dangerous. A real live wire. I didn't want to contact him with this sort of request unless it was absolutely necessary."

Felix smiled to himself. The ability to make grown men stutter was a gift that most didn't appreciate. It meant they didn't just fear him in the moment, but they feared what he could do in the future. Commander Lytes knew his future rested in Felix's hands. He'd been funding the Brotherhood for quite some time now. Even the Trid were in great debt to the entrepreneur. This would all pay off because he'd made the right friends. The enemy of his enemy was, well, not a friend, but an asset, to be sure.

"I don't have time to shiver over this supplier. I need names. If they have what I want, then we'll make a deal. Plain and simple," said, Felix, pulling his blue fedora hat from his head to reveal a scalp of smashed down gray hair.

"The Defiance may only deal with those they've dealt with before," explained Lytes. "I've had limited experience with them, many years ago, but I believe I can get in contact with them again."

"The Defiance, you say? I've heard of them. They've been quiet for some time." Felix was impressed. He had no idea the commander had such contacts.

"They've been lying low, operating mostly outside of the Federation's control."

"How cowardly of them. How are we supposed to overthrow the Federation if we don't create problems within their own space?" Felix asked, shaking his head.

Commander Lytes nodded, seeming to try again and again to swallow. "I agree. But the Defiance could resupply you," he continued. "The only problem will be setting up a meeting. We will need to handle things delicately, as they are rather quick to spook. Furthermore, you'll have to travel far outside Federation territory to meet with them, should they accept."

Felix laughed. "Creating a rebellion but being too afraid to do it inside of the colonies is pathetic. Sounds like I'll be doing their job for them by taking their weapons. What's the point in being defiant and not be in the enemy's face?"

Lytes nodded. "I'm sure they'll demand a great deal for the weapons, sir."

"I'm sure they will," agreed Felix. "But since they're cowards, we'll just wipe them out and take the weapons."

"W-Wipe them out, sir?" asked Commander Lytes.

"It will be a win-win," said Felix "I get my weapons and knock out a sad operation who can't cut it on their own." He sat down behind his desk. He was tired of cowards. Those who said they wanted to fight the fight but would hang around in safe territory. The Federation was here, and that's where he was going to be.

Until the bitter end.

"In that case, I'll set up a meeting for you, sir," said Commander Lytes.

"Yes, do that and quickly. I want my supply chamber filled as soon as possible. We'll be setting up a command base soon. The weapons will go there."

"You're moving fast now." Commander Lytes looked impressed and worried all at the same time.

"Of course, I am," said Felix, stroking the edge of his desk with his thumb. The cold metal surface was cool beneath his fingers. "I'm done hiding in the shadows. The time for action is now. I'm going on the offensive against the Federation." Felix Castile leaned forward, sharpening his eyes on the Kezzin before him. "General Lance has gone unpunished for far too long for what he did to us. To humanity. To the universe, itself. Soon, he'll meet his end, and all those who fight for him will be punished. I'm going to see to it." He dug his finger into the desk, chipping a splinter of the wood away. "Even if it kills me, I'll make them all pay."

FINIS

AUTHOR NOTES - SARAH NOFFKE

WRITTEN NOVEMBER 30, 2017

I wished I would have saved the log of questions I sent to MA when we were writing this book. I hope I didn't make his head hurt. The questions I sent MA went something like this:

"Is it possible to boost the boosters?"

"Can we call it a tri-rifle? Is that too simplistic?"

"Can we still call it a tri-rifle if Hatch makes it do four things?"

"Why don't you live closer? I need nachos."

That last one was after a long writing session of sprints. That's how I write the majority of the books. I set aside four to five hours in a day and sprint in thirty-minute increments with other authors. I used to think that sprinting was some sort of an ego game where authors tried to outdo each other's word counts. I've learned now, thanks to Facebook (aka time suck), that it's a way to stay focused. On the days I write alone, I'm like a new born puppy distracted by the shadows and ambient noises of a room. However, when I sprint with others, I'm committed to the craft. I can't goof off because putting up a three-hundred word total after a thirty minute sprint is sad. It meant I slacked off while other author friends pushed themselves. So that's how I get it done. There's no magic to it. No cigars and overflowing glasses of wine. Just sprint after sprint after sprint until I'm brain dead. Oh, and there's nachos. Some girls like chocolate, I like cheese.

You always get more than you bargained for with my author notes. Maybe way more than you wanted. Speaking of getting more than you bargained for. A huge thank you to James Caplan for all the help with the book. You went above and beyond to help with prose and your input is always valued.

When I was writing this book I ran out of drink names and calling it alcohol wasn't cutting it. So I polled the fans on Facebook, yes, there's a Facebook group and yes you can join. They supplied me with enough awesome names to keep me busy for the next dozen books. The flaming shots were named by Micky Cocker who brilliantly came up with baba yagas vengeance. And Thorsten Wiegand was the mastermind behind the Tullamore dew which was Chester's first whiskey. Oh, and because the fans are incredibly awesome and talented, I had one go so far as to write an entire description for the whiskey. A HUGE thank you to the creative prose offered by James Gartside for Dead Man Walking a Queens Bitch Space whiskey. That was probably my favorite part of the book, and I didn't even write it. Thank you to everyone for the suggestions. It's much more fun when you write the books for me. Keep your eyes peeled (honestly, I loathe that expression) because I will be using more suggestions from the fanbook group.

Okay, I'm told that I need to go and write book 3 because it's coming out soon. I'm going to take my shot of whiskey like a good girl and get to work. Thank you to you all for being amazing and not running from my ramblings.

Sarah

AUTHOR NOTES - MICHAEL ANDERLE

WRITTEN DECEMBER 3RD, 2017

First, let me say thank you for not only reading through the story but reading through Sarah's author notes to read mine as well!

Let me copy a couple of sentences from Sarah's author notes so that I can write a few of my thoughts I had when reading them for the first time.

First, we have:

"Can we still call it a tri-rifle if Hatch makes it do four things?"

And we follow it up with:

"Why don't you live closer? I need nachos."

One of the benefits of being the last person to write his author notes is seeing my collaborators and what they have written before me. I will admit when I read Sarah's sentences above; I laughed out loud. I can just imagine some of my characters (specifically anyone from Team BMW) asking that exact question, "Can we still call it a try rifle if Hatch makes it do four things?"

In my mind's eye, I sat there in thought about holding a barrel of a rifle (or something that has three barrels) with a perplexed look on my face when I realize it does four things and saying, "Why do they call it a Tri-rifle?"

I guess it just tickled my funny bone, and made me wonder again what would happen if we did some sort of field expedient modification to allow it to do *five* different things? The cynical side of me then starts asking questions such as, "Would the manufacturer's tried to sue someone for modifications which would cause the name to be useless?"

Occasionally, my cynical side needs to keep its mouth shut.

One of the challenges of writing up and down a timeline as we are now is when we have a situation in the second series, which hasn't been explained in the first series.

For example, I am writing some scenes this month with Ricky Bobby (an AI) which explains a situation that occurs in the first series, but shows up in their series decades (in the timeline) later.

I believe Sarah's book 03 will answer the question before my book Capture Death comes out on the 25th.

Or, at least I certainly hope so! If we put out the books and you STILL have questions? It means we failed to remember something that needs to be addressed and we will do our *best* to fix it.

(I should totally put in Sarah's email address here to answer all fans questions… But she would eventually figure out who had done this to her, and turnabout would be a bitch.)

It is so much fun to see characters that we dreamed up six months ago start resonating with fans. Hatch seems to be one of the early fan favorites. In your reviews on the book (should you choose to write one), would you let us know *which* character or characters are your favorites? I am not suggesting that I have any bets with any fellow collaborators on the results...

But if I get the information quicker, I might just set something up!

I hope you enjoy our series set in the Age of Expansion, the space opera/science fiction area of The Kurtherian Gambit.

May your December of this year, and your 2018, be fantastic!

Ad Aeternitatem,
Michael Anderle

ACKNOWLEDGMENTS

SARAH NOFFKE

Thank you to Michael Anderle for taking my calls and allowing me to play in this universe. It's been a blast since the beginning.

Thank you to Craig Martelle for cheering for me. I've learned so much working with you. This wild ride just keeps going and going.

Thank you to Jen, Tim, Steve, Andrew and Jeff for all the work on the books, covers and championing so much of the publishing.

Thank you to our beta team. I can't believe how fast you all can turn around books. The JIT team sometimes scares me, but usually just with how impressively knowledgeable they are.

Thank you to our amazing readers. I asked myself a question the other day and it had a strange answer. I asked if I would still write if trapped on a desert island and no one would ever read the books. The answer was yes, but the feeling connected to it was different. It wouldn't be as much fun to write if there wasn't awesome readers to share it with. Thank you.

Thank you to my friends and family for all the support and love.

THE GHOST SQUADRON

by Sarah Noffke and Michael Anderle

Formation (01)

Exploration (02)

Evolution (03)

Degeneration (04)

Impersonation (05)

Recollection (06)

WANT MORE?

ENTER

THE KURTHERIAN GAMBIT UNIVERSE

A desperate move by a dying alien race transforms the unknown world into an ever-expanding, paranormal, intergalactic force.

The Kurtherian Gambit Universe contains more than 100 titles in series created by Michael Anderle and many talented co-authors. For a complete list of books in this phenomenal marriage of paranormal and science fiction, go to:

http://kurtherianbooks.com/timeline-kurtherian/

ABOUT SARAH NOFFKE

Sarah Noffke, an Amazon Best Seller, writes YA and NA sci-fi fantasy, paranormal and urban fantasy. She is the author of the Lucidites, Reverians, Ren, Vagabond Circus, Olento Research and Soul Stone Mage series. Noffke holds a Masters of Management and teaches college business courses. Most of her students have no idea that she toils away her hours crafting fictional characters. Noffke's books are top rated and best-sellers on Kindle. Currently, she has eighteen novels published. Her books are available in paperback, audio and in Spanish, Portuguese and Italian.

SARAH NOFFKE SOCIAL

Website: http://www.sarahnoffke.com
Facebook: https://www.facebook.com/officialsarahnoffke
Amazon: http://amzn.to/1JGQjRn

BOOKS BY SARAH NOFFKE

THE SOUL STONE MAGE SERIES

House of Enchanted #1

The Kingdom of Virgo has lived in peace for thousands of years…until now.

The humans from Terran have always been real assholes to the witches of Virgo. Now a silent war is brewing, and the timing couldn't be worse. Princess Azure will soon be crowned queen of the Kingdom of Virgo.

In the Dark Forest a powerful potion-maker has been murdered.

Charmsgood was the only wizard who could stop a deadly virus plaguing Virgo. He also knew about the devastation the people from Terran had done to the forest.

Azure must protect her people. Mend the Dark Forest. Create alliances with savage beasts. No biggie, right?

But on coronation day everything changes. Princess Azure isn't who she thought she was and that's a big freaking problem.

Welcome to The Revelations of Oriceran.

The Dark Forest #2

Mountain of Truth #3

Land of Terran #4

New Egypt #5

Lancothy #6

THE LUCIDITES SERIES

Awoken, #1:

Around the world humans are hallucinating after sleepless nights. In a sterile, underground institute the forecasters keep reporting the same events. And in the backwoods of Texas, a sixteen-year-old girl is about to be caught up in a fierce, ethereal battle.

Meet Roya Stark. She drowns every night in her dreams, spends her hours reading classic literature to avoid her family's ridicule, and is prone to premonitions—which are becoming more frequent. And now her dreams are filled with strangers offering to reveal what she has always wanted to know: Who is she? That's the question that haunts her, and she's about to find out. But will Roya live to regret learning the truth?

Stunned, #2

Revived, #3

THE REVERIANS SERIES

Defects, #1

In the happy, clean community of Austin Valley, everything appears to be perfect. Seventeen-year-old Em Fuller, however, fears something is askew. Em is one of the new generation of Dream Travelers. For some reason, the gods have not seen fit to gift all of them with their expected special abilities. Em is a Defect—one of the unfortunate Dream Travelers not gifted with a psychic power. Desperate to do whatever it takes to earn her gift, she endures painful daily injections along with commands from her overbearing, loveless father. One of the few bright spots in her life is the return of a friend she had thought dead—but with his return comes the knowledge of a shocking, unforgivable truth. The society Em thought was protecting her has actually been betraying her, but she has no idea how to break away from its authority without hurting everyone she loves.

Rebels, #2

Warriors, #3

VAGABOND CIRCUS SERIES

Suspended, #1

When a stranger joins the cast of Vagabond Circus—a circus that is run by Dream Travelers and features real magic—mysterious events start happening. The once orderly grounds of the circus become riddled with hidden threats. And the ringmaster realizes not only are his circus and its magic at risk, but also his very life.

Vagabond Circus caters to the skeptics. Without skeptics, it would close its doors. This is because Vagabond Circus runs for two reasons and only two reasons: first and foremost to provide the lost and lonely Dream Travelers a place to be illustrious. And secondly, to show the nonbelievers that there's still magic in the world. If they believe, then they care, and if they care, then they don't destroy. They stop the small abuse that day-by-day breaks down humanity's spirit. If Vagabond Circus makes one skeptic believe in magic, then they halt the cycle, just a little bit. They allow a little more love into this world. That's Dr. Dave Raydon's mission. And that's why this ringmaster recruits. That's why he directs. That's why he puts on a show that makes people question their beliefs. He wants the world to believe in magic once again.

Paralyzed, #2

Released, #3

Ren: The Man Behind the Monster, #1

Born with the power to control minds, hypnotize others, and read thoughts, Ren Lewis, is certain of one thing: God made a mistake. No one should be born with so much power. A monster awoke in him the same year he received his gifts. At ten years old. A prepubescent boy with the ability to control others might merely abuse his powers, but Ren allowed it to corrupt him. And since he can have and do anything he wants, Ren should be happy. However, his journey teaches him that harboring so much power doesn't bring happiness, it steals it. Once this realization sets in, Ren makes up his mind to do the one thing that can bring his tortured soul some peace. He must kill the monster.

Note This book is NA and has strong language, violence and sexual references.

Ren: God's Little Monster, #2

Ren: The Monster Inside the Monster, #3

Ren: The Monster's Adventure, #3.5

Ren: The Monster's Death, #4

OLENTO RESEARCH SERIES

Alpha Wolf, #1:

Twelve men went missing.

Six months later they awake from drug-induced stupors to find themselves locked in a lab.

And on the night of a new moon, eleven of those men, possessed by new—and inhuman—powers, break out of their prison and race through the streets of Los Angeles until they disappear one by one into the night.

Olento Research wants its experiments back. Its CEO, Mika Lenna, will tear every city apart until he has his werewolves imprisoned once again. He didn't undertake a huge risk just to lose his would-be assassins.

However, the Lucidite Institute's main mission is to save the world from injustices. Now, it's Adelaide's job to find these mutated men and protect them and society, and fast. Already around the nation, wolflike men are being spotted. Attacks on innocent women are happening. And then, Adelaide realizes what her next step must be: She has to find the alpha wolf first. Only once she's located him can she stop whoever is behind this experiment to create wild beasts out of human beings.

Lone Wolf, #2

Rabid Wolf, #3

Bad Wolf, #4

BOOKS BY MICHAEL ANDERLE

For a complete list of books by Michael Anderle, go to:

www.lmbpn.com/ma-books

Audiobooks may be found at:

http://lmbpn.com/audible

CONNECT WITH MICHAEL ANDERLE

Website: http://kurtherianbooks.com/

Email List: http://kurtherianbooks.com/email-list/

Facebook Here:
https://www.facebook.com/TheKurtherianGambitBooks/

Printed in Great Britain
by Amazon